if mom's happy
STORIES OF EROTIC MOTHERS

EDITED BY
BRANDY FOX

Cwtch Press
Redmond, WA

Cwtch Press

16625 Redmond Way, Suite M-229

Redmond, WA 98052

www.cwtchpress.com

Print ISBN: 978-0-9969045-5-1

Cwtch Logo design by Elizabeth Person

Cover design & interior format by IndieDesignz.com

Previously Published Stories

"Pregnant Pause" by Jennifer D. Munro was originally published in *Shameless: Women's Intimate Erotica*, and also appeared in *The Erotica Writer's Husband & Other Stories*.

"Renewal" by Delilah Night was originally published in *Irresistible: Erotic Romance for Couples*.

"Waiting for Ilya" by Teresa Noelle Roberts was originally published in *Best Erotic Romance 2013*, and also appeared in *The Mammoth Book of Best New Erotica 12*.

"In the Early Morning Light" by Kristina Wright was originally published in *Curvy Girls*.

"Hook and Tink" by Brandy Fox was originally published in *The Mammoth Book of Quick & Dirty Erotica*.

contents

Introduction 1
by Brandy Fox
I Need Your Package 5
by Sara Dobie Bauer
Happy Mother's Day 17
by Jordan Monroe
In the Early Morning Light... 31
by Kristina Wright
Bills and Girls 39
by Samantha Luce
The Treadmill 47
by Brandy Fox
Tocks in My Ticker 53
by Pooja Pande
Mom's Night Out.. 59
by J.A. Reed
Pregnant Pause... 73
by Jennifer D. Munro
Renewal 79
by Delilah Night
A Desperate State.. 95
by Cecilia Duvalle
Waiting for Ilya.. 109
by Teresa Noelle Roberts
Toy Story 117
by Andrea Lani

Need 127
by Hollis Queens
Zap 135
by Luda Jones
Hook and Tink 147
by Brandy Fox
About the Authors.. 153
About the Editor 156

introduction

BRANDY FOX

The path through mothering affects nearly every aspect of sexuality: intimacy, identity, reproduction, body image, gender roles and expression, vulnerability, reciprocity, skin hunger, and so much more. Like great erotica, mothering explores the complexity of sexuality--the ache, the ecstasy, and everything in between.

It wasn't until I was knee-deep in mothering that I began reading and writing erotica. My reasons were as much about getting off as they were about hearing stories that evoke the human experience of sexuality. What I found to be lacking was the experience of mothers. This baffled me, given that at age forty, in the midst of a 15-year marriage with two kids, I was blindsided by a libido so intense, I had to start writing erotica just to channel those heart-pounding sexual fantasies hitting me full force any time of day: in the grocery store, at preschool parent meetings, even in Kindermusik class while singing *A Ram Sam Sam* across from an energetic teacher in a low-cut top. My sex drive insisted I pay attention to it, care for it, make time for it like I did my family. With a long-time partner, there were other benefits to a libido in overdrive: more time devoted to us as a couple, playing, connecting, letting go. It required frequent date nights, plotting and planning, sneaking and giggling, hushed orgasms that made the explosion all the more powerful, and loss of sleep that was well worth it. All this made the sex more fun, more delicious, and more satisfying.

Of course, it's not this way for all mothers. Some are healing from both natural and cesarean childbirth for months, even years. Some feel over-touched, as in Kristina Wright's "In the Early Morning Light":

Even the gentlest of touches, a hug or backrub, feels like sharp nails on a fresh sunburn. I don't want to be touched, but some part of me still longs for the connection of touch. To know I am more than a mother, a sometimes milk maker, a Frankenstein's monster of stretch marks and skin discolorations and numb flesh and that ugly scar.

The challenges continue long after our bodies heal and the kids toddle away. Juggling childcare with a job, house care, schoolwork, chauffeuring, and so much more can drain mothers of the playful, creative, giving energy required of sex.

In an ironic twist, studies show that women in their thirties and early forties are significantly more sexual than younger women. The result of this--or perhaps the cause--is that mothers are less inhibited, more in touch with their bodies, and more skilled at asking for what they want. They get right down to business and they know how to play--all traits of a great lover. That's why I've come to associate motherhood with totally hot sex. I have no doubt that you will, too, after reading these stories.

In these pages you will find women in all stages of motherhood navigating the complicated but essential path through--in some cases, back into--a healthy sex life. They're single, partnered, straight, queer, young, middle-aged, in the United States and abroad. But for all of them, sexuality is woven into the very fabric of mothering. Consider Pooja Pande's "Ticks in my Tocker," in which a mother is anticipating what she'll be doing later that night while putting her child to bed:

Some nights when I read Rasik his bedtime book, Dr. Seuss gets shaded dirty hues in my dirty mind. Like Mr. and Mrs. J. Carmichael Krox, I know that I've got ticks in my tocker and Sameer, tocks in his ticker. And I know that the reading of this book is the last PG-13 thing I'll be doing that night.

On the flipside, these women insist on weaving their job as mother into the fabric of their sexual identity. In Jordan Monroe's "Happy Mother's Day," for example, a new mother is dismayed that since having their first child, her husband treats her like a delicate flower. She concocts a kinky plan to remind him of what turns her on, and the results are intensely hot.

Whether it's long-overdue self-care or just a good hard fuck they're after; the delivery man, their former student, or their spouse of twenty-years; in their own home, a hotel room, the tattoo parlor, or the gym; every mother in these pages knows how to arouse and be aroused. No matter where, when, or how, these stories capture the complex and profound--and ultimately satisfying--task of attending to your own desires while tending to children.

Brandy Fox
Seattle, Washington

i need your package

SARA DOBIE BAUER

Hannah once saw her delivery man carry a big screen television under one arm. Another time, it was a dining room table from IKEA. You'd never guess, looking at the guy. He was tall and slim but not *bulging*. His long appendages probably helped, as did his sense of balance. He could stand on one foot like a yogi in tree pose—big box leaned on top of his thigh, scanner in the other. Like a ballet dancer, he jumped off porches and back into his big, brown truck. Hannah could hear that truck coming from three blocks away.

Dayton usually stopped at Hannah's house around 11 AM. At 10:30, she successfully coaxed the baby into a nap. She made sure her blonde hair was in a respectable ponytail. Changing out of her robe, she put on a sweater that flared at the waist and jeans that didn't look too "Mommy."

If only she were so in tune with her own child.

Baby Neely had been mostly her husband's idea. They'd discussed having children early in their marriage, but their careers got in the way. Hannah reviewed books for a mainstream women's website; her husband worked early hours, often on the road. Then, at the age of thirty-six, it just sort of happened. Neely happened.

Hannah heard the rumble of Dayton's truck and felt the way the sound vibrated in her chest. She scampered to the door and pulled it open, its old hinges squeaking just enough to wake Neely, who started wailing upstairs.

"Shit," she whispered but pasted on a smile when Dayton jumped gracefully onto her porch with three separate yellow envelopes under his arm.

"Good morning, Hannah." He winked one of his hazel eyes.

"Morning." She gawked up at him and hoped her irises weren't in the shape of hearts.

The scanner beeped as he ran it over the label of each individually wrapped book from publishers who desperately wanted her opinion. "Did you want me to fuck you on the porch next time?"

Her hand flew to her chest. "I'm sorry?"

"Did you want me to leave these on the porch next time? I don't want to wake the baby." The late autumn sun reflected off his short, auburn hair. His presence mimicked the fallen leaves in her front yard: those green-gold eyes, hair almost red, and slim fitting brown uniform.

"No, it's fine. She just needs to be fed."

"Oh, right."

Did he glance down at her chest? Hannah had the urge to grab the back of his head and shove his face against her aching breasts. Then again, how sexy was a padded nursing bra?

"Well." He handed her the packages. "See you later." His smile was crooked and went up much higher on the right than left.

Hannah watched him go. Well, she watched his ass go until he hopped into the front seat of his truck, turned the ignition, and sent another vibration of sound … right to her clit.

Six weeks after the baby, and her body still wasn't her own. Hannah hadn't put on a horrific amount of weight during the pregnancy, but it was obvious she'd had a baby. Her stretched-out abdomen pressed full and tight against maternity jeans. Her once B-cup breasts were double D balloons that ached half the time. The worst was what Neely's over-sized head had done on its way out, which was why she and her husband had yet to have sex since the baby.

Which was why Hannah's deliveryman had become such a fascination.

~

She sat and considered: what kind of name was Dayton anyway?

On the couch, she bounced Neely up and down. The baby cooed and stared at her mother. She had her father's eyes but white-gold hair like Hannah's. She bounced Neely some more until the little girl reached up and tugged Hannah's hair. Hannah screeched, which made the baby cry.

"I'm sorry." She sighed and pulled Neely into a hug. Drool soaked the shoulder of her t-shirt. She held Neely back enough to wipe her mouth with Hannah's nearby sweater. Ever since having the baby, her body temperature had been volatile. One second, she was cold; the next, it was like someone tossed her ass into Hell—which was a pretty good metaphor for her opinion of motherhood so far, hot and cold. She loved her little girl and the way her skin smelled sweet. She loved her tiny, pudgy fingers. But Hannah missed freedom. She missed sex, and it wasn't her husband's fault. Hannah was the one who felt pudgy, soft, and exhausted.

She'd masturbated that morning for the first time since giving birth. She'd almost passed out from the pleasure, thinking about Dayton's bright hazel eyes and the way his hidden superhero strength would make the bedroom into an amusement park ride. In the fantasy, he even kept on his big, brown boots, but it was just a fantasy. Who would want her like this?

Neely pulled Hannah's hair again, then sucked a couple pieces into her tiny mouth.

Hannah tugged her hair away. "What's that, Dayton? Oh, it's called Eau de Drool. A new fragrance, sprung from my stretched out cooch."

She carried Neely to the kitchen and retrieved a bottle of milk. The bottles had so far saved Hannah's nipples from constant torture, although Neely did prefer the fresh stuff. Just as she prepared to return to her couch—and try to skim a couple of the review copies Dayton had delivered the day before—someone knocked on her front door. Strange, it was only 9:30.

She put the bottle down and waddled with baby. Looking out the peephole, she ducked as though Dayton the deliveryman might be able to see through walls. What the hell was he doing there so early? She was in a robe! She hadn't even brushed her teeth!

"Hannah?" His voice reminded her of his big, vibrating truck.

Neely squeaked at the sound of his voice, surely loud enough for him to hear.

"Oh, thanks a lot, kid," Hannah muttered. "Just a minute!" she said aloud. She did a quick glance in the antique vanity by the front door and tried to ignore the dark circles under her eyes.

He gifted her with a crooked grin when she opened the door, the sun barely above the trees across the street. Neely reached one limp arm out toward the man on the porch.

Yeah, I know what you mean.

"May I?" he asked, setting down a bouquet of red roses.

"Uh, sure."

He held the baby like he knew what he was doing. "Forgive me, but I don't actually have a package for you."

"Oh."

"I just thought you looked like you needed flowers." He nudged the bouquet with the tip of his brown boot, and Hannah blushed when she flashed back to her earlier imaginings of what he'd look like in nothing but.

"You brought me flowers?"

"Better than all those books, right?" He made a funny face at Neely, which brought out deep laugh wrinkles around his eyes. Hannah suspected he wasn't as young as his bearing implied. He was probably her age, in fact. The sparse brown hairs on his forearms shined as the sun surmounted trees.

"Well, thank you, Dayton."

"You're very welcome, Hannah."

"Do you give all the sad, pathetic moms in the neighborhood flowers or just me?"

He rocked Neely. "I don't think you're pathetic, and I didn't know you were sad. Are you sad?"

"I guess not."

"But something's wrong."

She shrugged. "I miss sex."

"Oh." His mouth made the most adorable round shape, and just as quickly, his bright eyes darted to her left hand. Hannah didn't have on her wedding band. Her fingers felt too swollen.

"I didn't mean …"

"I didn't assume." He winked.

"Are you married?"

"I am," he said.

"Happily?"

"Very." With one hand holding Neely, he brought his other up and bopped the baby on the nose. She flashed little baby gums.

"So what would your wife think about you bringing a bouquet of red roses to some stranger?"

"We're not strangers. I'm your deliveryman." He leaned forward to hand Neely back, and Hannah felt her nursing bra dampen when their arms touched.

She turned a moan into a cough.

Dayton leaned over and picked up the flowers before holding them out to her. Hannah smiled politely and started backing into her house, but before she could, he took a step forward and pressed a gentle kiss to the side of her mouth.

"Get some rest," he whispered. His breath smelled like cinnamon gum. Whistling, he turned and walked back to his truck.

⌇

Was she supposed to throw away the roses? She put them in a vase in Neely's room next to the baby's crib. Then, she stood above her sweet little girl and ran her fingertips over the silken hair on top of her vulnerable head.

Hannah felt sort of like a baby's skull—fragile, not quite formed, in need of cushioning. She'd like to be cushioned right between Dayton's pecs, in fact. She rubbed at the wrinkles on her forehead, furrowed since he'd left. She wanted to sleep. She wanted to get lost in a great book. She wanted to be fucked into the mattress. Hell, fucked against a wall. She just wanted to feel *wanted*.

Against her better judgment, she stepped in front of the cutesy full-length mirror in Neely's room, painted in pastel zoo animals, and groaned. Whoever said new mothers glowed was full of shit.

She didn't glow; she sucked light from the room, devoured the sun with her own exhaustion. Her once brilliant hair fell in flat planes around her puffy face. Red streaks rimmed her brown eyes, accented by purple circles beneath. Her breasts were like huge boulders, and her stomach was a half-deflated beach ball.

No wonder she was dreaming of the deliveryman. She'd been reading too many Bridget Jones wannabe books—the ones where the awkward, unattractive girl gets the hot guy based on charm alone. Well, Hannah was too tired to be charming, and she certainly didn't deserve a guy who looked like Dayton.

In silence, she cried, scared of waking Neely. She carried the baby monitor downstairs and sank into the couch, wiping tears from her face. A woodpecker gave some quick taps to one of the big trees in her backyard. The bird stopped and tapped some more, which was when Hannah realized the tapping wasn't coming from a tree but from her front door.

In fluffy socks, she tiptoed to the entrance and opened the door a crack.

One of Dayton's cheekbones stared back at her, his eyes looking off down the street. At the sound of the door opening, he turned toward her.

"What are you doing here?" she whispered.

"Giving you what you need." He pushed the door open gently and stepped into her foyer. He still smelled of cinnamon but there were other scents, too: that of paper and packing tape and a touch of sweat.

"But—"

Before she could argue, he backed her against the wall and kissed her neck. She shoved at his shoulders … then pulled on his shoulders.

"The baby is sleeping."

He smiled. "Then we'll have to be very quiet." He went back to kissing her neck, followed by her collarbone. His large hands pushed her robe open, revealing a less than sexy cotton nightgown.

"I'm not ..." She blushed and pulled the robe closed. "Dayton, I'm not ... You don't want me like this. Look at you." She ran her thumb over his bottom lip, her hand up into his hair.

"Look at *you*." He pushed the robe open again and kissed her right on the mouth. "Your soft curves and the smell of baby powder." He pressed his knee between her legs. "I want to bury myself in you. Please."

Hannah tried to catch her breath but lost herself grinding against his knee.

"I take that as a yes?"

"Mm."

He picked her up with ease like one of his heavy packages and carried her to the couch. When he reached to unbutton his shirt, she shook her head and beckoned him closer.

"I've been thinking about tearing this uniform off you for weeks."

He licked his lips and watched as she tugged buttons loose, revealing a muscular chest and smattering of light hair. When she sucked his nipple, he groaned, but Hannah covered his mouth.

"The baby."

"Sorry." He removed the unbuttoned brown shirt from his shoulders and threw it on the floor before lying on top of her. Again, he went for her mouth, paying more attention to her lips and even sucking her tongue.

She tugged his hair. "God, Dayton, more ..."

"What do you want?"

"I need you to fuck me right now."

One of his eyebrows went up. "You're sure?"

"Now." She unlatched his belt buckle and unzipped his pants before shoving the fabric off his ass, along with his underwear. His cock sprung up between them. Talk about a package ready for delivery… She took it in her palm and rubbed up and down, reveling in the way his eyes closed and his mouth opened in a silent plea.

He allowed himself to be toyed with but not for long. Soon, he lifted the bottom of her nightgown and pressed her thighs apart.

For a second—merely a second—Hannah felt hesitant. She knew she had a bit of scarring down there. She hadn't been penetrated since her daughter's birth. Would it hurt when he pushed inside?

Dayton must have noticed, because he stopped moving. She looked up to find him staring, cheeks flushed. "We don't have to do this right now."

"Yes. We do." She grabbed his face and pulled him against her. "But first we need coconut oil."

"Coconut oil?"

"On the counter by the stove."

"Right." He tugged up his pants enough to walk to her kitchen before hurrying back with a small glass jar.

She snatched it away from him and spun the top. The smell of pina coladas mixed with sex as she spread a liberal amount on his junk and between her legs. He almost fell right on top of her when she wrapped her ankle around the back of his knee, but he caught himself with his hands and lingered above her.

"Now, fuck me, deliveryman. Fuck me hard."

"You keep talking like that, and this is gonna be over way too fast."

He guided himself to her entrance, an area Hannah now considered unfamiliar. She closed her eyes as he pushed inside but felt no pain. After so many weeks without sex, she felt a sense of awe at the newness of him. His excessive girth made her back arch, as did his adherence to fucking her practically through the furniture.

She had to press a throw pillow against her face as he continued pounding, and she stuck her own fingers in his mouth to stop him from shouting as he came. Her own orgasm smashed into her seconds later, and she screamed loud and hard into that cheap rayon square from Pier I.

He collapsed on top of her, and she giggled when she realized he really had kept on his boots. Dayton didn't get up, just nuzzled his nose against her neck. She couldn't even lift her arms.

"Oh, I needed that," she murmured.

"Me, too," he said. "I love you."

"I love you, too, sweetie."

"Can we stop pretending I'm not your husband now?"

She chuckled into his hair. "Yes. But wasn't it fun playing a little game?"

He haltingly lifted himself onto one elbow. "I don't need to play games with you, Hannah."

She tugged his chest hair. "I thought it would be exciting to make me something forbidden. Make me more desirable."

His eyebrows lowered. "There is no one more desirable to me than you."

She rolled her eyes. "Not like this." She put her hand on her puffy stomach.

He put his hand over hers. "Exactly like this. Not only are you the career woman I've always loved, but now, you're also the mother of my child. Plus, your tits are huge."

She laughed, which managed to wake Neely. The baby's bellows echoed down their creaky century-old home stairs.

"Now we're in trouble." Dayton rolled off her and stood. He

pulled his pants up but not before Hannah gave him a good smack on the ass. "I'll get her." He grabbed his shirt before hurrying up the steps, his boots clunking with every leap.

She pulled her nightgown back down as dampness dripped between her legs. Not the sexiest sensation, and yet, in that moment, she wouldn't trade that magical mix of her husband and makeshift lube. Soon, he came back downstairs with their little girl in his arms—their little girl with her father's hazel eyes and her mother's bright blonde hair. Neely's face leaned against Dayton's chest as her tiny hands curled against his uniform.

"Tell me you're not sad, Hannah. With me." He kissed Neely's head. "With us." He looked up at her from beneath light eyelashes—handsome as the day they met.

"Just keep delivering my packages, big boy." She winked.

happy mother's day

JORDAN MONROE

Theresa's cell phone dimly illuminated the master bedroom. *Gloria is with Grandma and Grandpa. Should be home in twenty minutes.*

Can't wait to be with you. XOXO, she responded with a kissing emoji.

They'd discussed this night time and time again. They'd agreed on boundaries, safewords, and acceptable stopping points. They both knew there could be consequences, knowing the risk of jealousy would be present. A potent blend of trepidation and excitement coursed through her.

She tightened her scarlet silk robe and walked into their master bathroom. In preparation for the evening, Kyle had arranged her a spa day, while he had cleaned the house top to bottom. Both the kitchen and master bathroom were spotless, the living room devoid of baby toys, and Gloria's crib tucked away in the spare bedroom. The only time the house had been this clean was before they'd hosted their housewarming.

Theresa turned on the bathroom light and stood in front of the mirror, opening her robe to survey her changed, naked body.

The hairdresser had styled her chocolate brown hair in loose waves that fell past her shoulders; she'd taken to tying it back and out of the way, one less distraction from her busy days as a new mother. She'd swept on a coat of deep red lipstick and coated her lashes with mascara, making her face more sultry and reminiscent of that time before her life revolved around nothing but folic acid and child proof locks. Theresa smiled back at herself, a gentle smile so as to not break out into a series of laugh lines and crow's feet. The effect was pleasant enough.

Her eyes traveled down her body, past her neck which she moisturized religiously, and stopped at her breasts. She'd always had a full chest, but the pregnancy hormones had caused them to swell to an almost cartoonish size. Her nipples, once the locus of foreplay, had been sore from Gloria's incessant nursing.

On the shared sink, there was a jar of organic cocoa butter one of her colleagues had discreetly given her at her baby shower. Theresa opened the bottle and rubbed some between her fingers, warming it up. With both hands, she massaged her areolas and nipples, coating them with moisturizer. She watched herself in the mirror and felt a river of warmth trickle down within her body. Theresa gently pulled at both her nipples, recognizing the familiar electric tug radiating from them. They weren't sore anymore.

She tugged at them again, twisting as she pinched. The sensation was sharper this time. Biting her lower lip, she repeated the gesture, losing herself in the blissful, physical moments.

She looked at her lower body, trying to ignore the small paunch that didn't care how many crunches she did daily. At the spa earlier that day, Theresa had splurged on a bikini wax. Her pubic hair was now a neat, dark brown triangle, her lips completely waxed. She snaked her right hand down to her center, easing her fingers into that most private of places. The pad of her middle finger brushed against the swollen nub of her clit, and she gasped. The shock was both new and familiar, like a set of muscles that hadn't been worked in years suddenly getting back into shape. She brushed it again, curling her pedicured toes under her feet. A new flood of warmth rushed through her body, terminating at that exact spot.

The guilt she now felt wasn't a new emotion. Ever since Gloria's birth, Theresa and Kyle had thrown themselves into parenthood. Though not perfect, Kyle had turned out to be as exceptional a father as he was a husband: affectionate, resourceful, calm, and eager to help. He'd taken to splitting chores like a fish to water, which hadn't surprised Theresa: he was more in tune with the domestic side of life, while she was more suited to the cerebral and the budgetary aspects of it. Despite all of this, their physical passion had waned dramatically; the recovery from pregnancy had not been easy on Theresa, and though she wanted nothing more than to be as hot and sweaty as they had been before becoming parents, the physical trauma had rendered that a distant wish. Because of this, however, Kyle had taken to treating her like a delicate flower for the six months since their child's birth. This deeply troubled her.

She straightened up and closed the robe around her. Her nipples were showing through the silk provocatively. Her mouth curled into a smile.

"Honey, I'm home!"

Theresa heard the clatter of keys hitting the granite countertop and the shrug of a puffer coat coming off her husband's shoulders. She ran her fingers through her hair one last time, doing her best to make her tresses as voluminous as possible. She went into their bedroom and turned down the dimmer lights. Her grandmother had suggested using soft pink bulbs in the bedroom: "It's the most flattering light, my dear. Disguises every flaw," she'd told her with a wink.

Lowering the pitch in her voice in an attempt at sensuality, she called down to him. "I'm waiting in the bedroom."

The slow, deliberate cadence of his footsteps up the stairs caused her pulse to race. She lay on her side, propping her head up with her left hand. Recalling all those silly romance novels she'd read in high school, Theresa was trying to channel the archetypal seductress. On this night, her most desperate desire was to devastate her husband with a single, heavy-lidded stare.

As his shadow crossed the hallway wall, her breath stopped. With languid steps, Kyle entered the room. He stopped at the edge of the bed, staring at her with dark, wide eyes. She watched him swallow. "What do you think, Kyle?"

He tucked his hands in his pockets, as though she were a masterpiece and he did not wish to ruin the illusion. "You're perfect, Theresa."

She smiled, this time not caring about wrinkles. "Do you think he'll like it?"

"He'd be an idiot not to like it. When's he expected?"

"About ten minutes. You should get prepared."

"You think so?" He raised an eyebrow.

She gave him the satisfaction of a stern order. "Yes. I didn't stutter."

Bowing his head, he muttered, "Yes ma'am."

She followed him with her eyes as he quickly walked into their bathroom and closed the door. Theresa released the breath that she'd been holding. She hadn't tapped into her dominating side for a long time, and it had taken a great deal of mental energy to get there. Sitting up on the bed, she reached for her phone again. There was a new text message.

I will be there in five minutes. Can't wait to play. Will he be secured?

She grinned and typed back, *Wonderful. Yes, he will be secured. Would you like a drink upon arrival?*

Ice water will be much appreciated.

With that, Theresa turned off her phone and placed it in the nightstand. The bathroom door opened, and her husband, wearing nothing save for black boxer briefs, emerged. She allowed herself time to gaze at Kyle. He was tall, towering over her, his face chiseled with delicate bone structure, his dark hair cut short and close, reminiscent of Julius Caesar. In his collegiate days, he'd been on the cross-country team, and the few significant bulges on his lean body were centered on his hips. She held his gaze, waiting for him to lower his eyes in reverence.

Theresa walked over to him and stroked his cheek. "Look at me."

On command, he raised his eyes, looking down into hers. She stood on tiptoes and kissed his stubbled cheek. "No matter what happens, know that I am forever yours."

He closed his eyes and leaned his face into her hand. "I know. I love you, Theresa."

"Good. Go sit down."

She swatted her husband's ass as he walked to the antique chair between the bed and the window. When he was seated, Theresa dug around her nightstand and pulled out the item chosen for this night: a pair of thick, leather handcuffs. She walked over to him, straddling his legs, letting the robe fall open. She leaned forward, the heat of his body radiating onto her nipples, daring him to touch her. "Give me your wrists."

Kyle did as he was instructed, and Theresa carefully slipped the cuffs over each wrist. He tested them, trying to pull them apart. When they wouldn't give, she asked him, "Are you comfortable?"

He nodded. Kyle had slipped into his submissive role quite readily. She was still mentally preparing. This was a first for both of them, after all.

"Good. I'll be right back. Don't move from the chair. Do not use the switch to release yourself." The cuffs came with a mechanism for the wearer to remove, should the need arise.

With that, she kissed his lips, coaxing them open with her tongue, receiving her husband's familiar and exquisite taste. Before she got lost in the kiss, she broke away and headed downstairs.

As though it had been staged, the doorbell rang. After arranging her robe so that only the swell of her breasts was exposed, Theresa opened the front door. She smiled. "Hi, Sam. It's good to see you."

She stood aside, letting Sam cross the threshold into the house. As she offered to take his jacket, she allowed herself to stare at him. Her former lover was as tall as her husband, but their similarities ended there. Sam was solid, as though hewn from stone, his muscles rippling from one to the next. She hung his jacket up in the hall closet, silently urging him to follow her into the kitchen. Theresa released a sigh of gratitude, seeing that Kyle had squirreled Gloria's highchair out of sight.

After getting a plastic cup from the cabinet, Theresa dropped ice cubes in it, then filled the cup with filtered water and handed it to Sam. "Your drink, as requested."

He took it, their fingers barely touching, yet it was enough for Theresa's senses to heighten. Sam lowered his massive body into one of their kitchen chairs, looking out of place against the oak wood and the floral seat cushions. Under his piercing gaze, Theresa felt terribly vulnerable, but she did not shy away. She noted that his beard had grown fuller, with occasional streaks of grey amidst the sea of dark hair. His grey eyes sparkled with intent; Theresa could only guess what he had planned for her.

At last he spoke. "Is he restrained upstairs?"

The rich, deep timbre of his voice rumbled through her, opening familiar fault lines deep within her psyche. "He is, yes."

Sam took another drink of water. Theresa watched his full, pink lips cover the rim of the glass, wishing they were on her skin. He swallowed and stated, "As we have discussed, if you speak to me, address me as Sir. Nothing else. The safeword that we are all to use is 'daisies.' Anal play is a hard limit. Use of the term, 'bitch' is a hard limit. Unless I request otherwise, you are to look at your husband at all times. I will wear a condom. Upon completion of tonight's events, I will shower and leave. Your husband will handle aftercare. Do you have any questions?"

"No. No, Sir," she quickly corrected.

Another sip of water. "How are you feeling, Theresa?"

"I'm feeling just fine."

He shot her a serious look. "I may not be your lover anymore, but I still know when you are lying. I'll ask again: how are you feeling?"

She rolled her eyes and shifted on her feet, suddenly uncomfortable. She had to choose her words carefully, pinpointing the emotions and articulating them with accuracy. "Motherhood is tiresome. I have to struggle each day to find the joy in it. Kyle, on the other hand, is a tremendous father. I always had a feeling that he would be, but I'm quite shocked at how taken he is with it."

Sam took a final swig, then set the cup on the table. The ice cubes loudly clattered against each other. He leaned forward, continuing to stare at her, daring her to reveal more of her inner workings. "What else, Theresa?"

She looked down at herself. The robe was dangerously close to opening completely, yet she did not move to close it. In a faint whisper, she answered, "I miss being objectified."

"Go on."

The words rapidly escaped her lips. "I miss the way Kyle used to look at me. The way you used to look at me. The way *men* used to look at me. I know many women hate the leers, and most of the time I hate them as well, but sometimes I want my husband to salivate and attack me, to lose control with me. Ever since I got pregnant, Kyle has been so infuriatingly gentle with me. I want him to *own* me again." She took a deep breath, in an attempt to calm herself.

A silence hung in the air. After a pause, Sam replied, "We'll get him there. Consider that my Mother's Day gift."

She looked at the grin on his face and felt herself relax. The three of them hadn't discussed whether this would be a permanent arrangement; Theresa was hoping tonight would be enough.

"I'm glad you're smiling, Theresa. Come here and sit astride me," he said flatly.

Theresa crossed over to the kitchen chair, placed her hands on Sam's shoulders, and sat on his lap. The heat between her legs was exposed to him. Sam wrapped his left arm around her waist, and she knew it would do no good to resist his strength. With his right hand, he delicately peeled the edges of her robe back from her body. The soft hairs of his beard tickled her skin in the most familiar yet unexpected way.

She looked down at him, noting how he basely stared at her swollen breasts. Without looking up at her, he asked, "I take it you're nursing?"

"I am, so there's no need for a lecture on the benefits of breastfeeding."

His hold around her waist tightened. She sucked air through her teeth, rapidly warming to the way he took control of her. "Do you want your breasts to be touched?"

The way he punctuated the consonants while letting the words linger on his tongue was enough to make Theresa toss her head back and moan. She loved being spoken to so objectively.

To her disappointment, she didn't feel the warmth of his hands on her. Theresa opened her eyes and watched as Sam reached for his water glass, shook up the remaining ice cubes, and placed one in his mouth. Her jaw went slack. Before she could say anything, his lips covered her right nipple.

Her fingers threaded through his thick, dark hair and she rocked her hips into him as he flicked his tongue over it. She was keenly aware of each sensation, her body tightening as her nipple puckered. When it was at its hardest, Theresa felt the brutal shock of the ice on her skin.

She cried out and tried to wriggle away, but Sam held her to him, growling a little as he tightened his hold. Theresa felt him alternate between soothing warmth and wicked cold on her nipple, and she craved everything he gave. Looking down, she watched as Sam's hand closed over her left breast, his fingers teasing the tip until it puckered. He pulled at it as he laved ice water over her other nipple, the combination becoming unbearable. She desperately didn't want this to end, but was embarrassed for what was surely about to—

"Shit, I'm so sorry," she said as she let go of his head and tried to move away from his grasp. He released her, and she leapt off of him, looking at the milk trickling down her belly. She flattened her palms and made to wipe it away.

"Don't do that. Let's go upstairs."

She raised her head to look at Sam, unable to read his expression. He rose from the chair and stood behind her, swatting her ass. She yelped and started walking towards the stairs. She tried not be feel embarrassed about the breast milk trickling down her front, and hated this reminder of her changed self.

Theresa led Sam into the bedroom. Kyle remained seated in the chair, his wrists still imprisoned by the cuffs.

Sam's hand was against the small of her back, pushing her towards her husband. "Take off the robe, Theresa."

With shaking hands, she grasped the edges of the robe and let it fall from her shoulders. She stood naked in the middle of the room, one foot behind the other, doing her best to radiate confidence when really she was mortified at the mess on her torso. Again, Sam pushed her towards Kyle. When her legs touched her husband's, she sensed that Sam was not satisfied.

"Straddle him."

She did as she was told. Kyle inhaled sharply. She welcomed his familiar warmth, his long and tight body, his clean scent. His breath tickled her sensitive flesh.

"She leaked. Lick it off of her."

Theresa looked over her shoulder at Sam, shocked at his statement. Before she could protest, she felt the moist warmth of Kyle's tongue on her skin. Her legs went weak, and she collapsed on top of him, grinding her hips into his growing hardness. Her milk had streamed down her body, and Kyle lapped up every drop. The tenderness he displayed, particularly in this depraved act, shot through Theresa. This was exactly what she desired.

When Kyle finished, Sam's voice cut through the room. "Remove yourself from him, Theresa."

She looked down into her husband's eyes, noticing the white-hot, penetrative desire in them. He dutifully remained in the chair, though Theresa noticed his knuckles were white as he clenched his hands into fists. She smiled: he wanted her with him.

"Lie down on the bed. On your back. Do not look at me."

As instructed, she kept her eyes trained on her husband. They communicated to each other by sight alone. She heard Sam start to remove his clothing, and she swallowed. Between his legs, she could see Kyle's erection straining against the cotton of his underwear. She looked back up to his face, noticing that his jaw had gone slack. Even in the dim light, she could see his neat white teeth. For this moment in time, his attention was solely on her.

She drank it in.

The bed gave to Sam's weight. A gasp escaped her as his beard hairs tickled her flesh and he inched his way up her body. His chest hair followed, and she was soon covered by this large, hairy, intensely masculine man. Her eyes rolled back as his hand clasped her neck.

"Do you like to be handled this way, Theresa?"

With a struggle, she whispered, "Yes."

For her response, she was rewarded with a series of kisses along her neck. Sam rained feather-light brushes of his lips down her collarbone, ending at the center of her breasts. He leaned up, asking, "Kyle, what does your wife's breast milk taste like? Describe it to me."

It was such an overtly sexual question, coming from him. There was a part of her that didn't want to know, and another part of her that desperately wanted to hear her husband's answer. "It's sweet and creamy. I'd definitely try another taste."

"Before you do, though, I'm going to taste her milk."

Releasing his hold from her neck, Sam swung one of his legs over Theresa's body. She felt his erection, aggressive and demanding, near her center. She tilted her hips up towards it, wanting to feel more of him. Her motions were stopped, though, as he grasped both of her breasts and pushed them together so that her nipples touched. She moaned when Sam lowered his head and drew upon both of her nipples, teasing each with his tongue. Again, she threaded her fingers through Sam's hair and writhed against him, the sensations making her lose all sense of control. Warm liquid dripped down the side of her breasts: she'd lactated again.

"You're right. Sweet and creamy," Sam muttered as he drank from her.

Every ounce of strength in her body had been sapped because of the attention both of these men had paid her. Her legs seem to fall open as Sam snaked one arm down her body. She sighed as his fingers toyed with her inner folds, coating his fingertips with her slick arousal. Theresa rocked her hips against the pressure, wanting everything he gave her.

Sam released her nipples from his mouth and leaned back. Looking at Kyle, he said, "Seems your wife is ready for me. Shall I give her what she wants?"

Theresa opened her eyes to look at her husband. His chest was rising and falling, as though he'd run a sprint. His cock was nearly bursting from his underwear. "Dear God, yes," he said with a strained voice.

Sam left the bed again, but Theresa did not watch him. She searched Kyle's face for meaning. Was there jealousy? Rage? Pain? The only expression she could clearly read on his face was that of pure lust. She breathed a heavy sigh of relief.

Sam was back on the bed. Theresa bit down on her lower lip when she felt the tip of his thick cock tease her folds, another familiar yet foreign feeling. She pushed her hips up towards him again, still looking at her husband. She wanted to see his face while another man entered her. When she felt Sam's cock inch inside her, teasing her, she reached up and grasped the headboard. Finally, with one devastating thrust, he filled her completely; it was only at that moment that she was unable to look at her husband.

Sam knelt and held her legs around his waist, lifting her lower body off the bed. Through his fucking, Theresa recognized what he was doing. He was putting his actions on display before her husband. She had wanted Kyle to see her as the sexual creature she'd always been, and Sam had only been too happy to oblige. The thought sent a different wave flooding over her. A drop of fluid escaped her and dripped down to her private, puckered hole. Her eyes slammed shut.

She groaned as Sam's fingertips brushed against her clit, never stopping his movements. He continued rocking against her, making her entire body a pool to receive pleasure. Little sounds escaped from her lips, as though she were begging Sam to continue without using words.

"Look at Kyle, Theresa. Look at him."

Wrenching her eyes open, she twisted her head towards Kyle. Out of her peripheral vision, she could see the muscles in Sam's torso flex as he pounded into her. She could even see the trickles of sweat curling from his neck and down his chest. Training her eyes on Kyle, she saw his hands were in his lap, unmoving. He was still very much alert to her. She looked into his eyes, and recognized the question in them.

"You may touch yourself, Kyle," she panted as Sam's thrusts became harder against her.

She watched as Kyle's fingers worked the fabric of his underwear, revealing his rigid, perfect cock. When he grasped it, she licked her lips. *This* had been what she wanted: her husband to really see her, to know that she could still be the full-bodied, libidinous woman she was before bringing life into the world. Kyle quickened his strokes. Theresa heard her husband's breath become shallow and strained. His orgasm was imminent.

Theresa was suddenly flooded with urgency. She wanted to feel her husband's hands on her while this other man reduced her. With a cry of pleasure, she said, "Take off the cuffs, Kyle, and put your hands on me."

Sam didn't say anything, continuing his exacting, wonderful rhythm. Immediately, Kyle was next to her, both of his warm hands covering her breasts. He massaged them, and Theresa looked into his eyes. The tenderness was still there, but was joined by a lascivious gleam. She knew that he wanted to take pleasure as much as he wanted to give.

Releasing the headboard, she reached down and wrapped her fingers around Kyle's white-hot length. He groaned, but did not stop kneading her breasts. With pinches that were close to painful, he pulled at her nipples. Again, her milk leaked from them, but this time she didn't mind. Kyle rubbed the fluid over her skin, which sent another spray out from her nipples.

It was becoming too much. She was right on the edge of collapsing. As though the three of them shared a thought, she felt Sam's thumb on her clit, moving in tiny circles. Kyle closed his lips over her left nipple and sucked, grazing his teeth over it.

"I'm coming! I'm coming!" She screamed and writhed against both of them, losing herself. Sam shuddered, thrust a few more times into her, and stilled. Finally, she nodded at Kyle, who shot a jet of his essence onto her now soaking breasts.

After a brief, silent moment, Sam removed himself from her. "Can I use the shower in here?"

"By all means," Theresa whispered. "Red towel is for you."

"Thank you." With that, he closed the bathroom door, leaving the couple on the bed.

Kyle lay down next to her. She knew she must look a disaster: her hair was in disarray, and her body was slathered in multiple fluids.

As though he'd read her mind and wanted to dispel her of that notion, he covered her lips with his. There was so much that needed to be said, but in that single kiss, Theresa knew that there would be no further need of Sam's presence in their marital bed.

in the early morning light

KRISTINA WRIGHT

This is how it begins: me lying in bed just before dawn, woozy from lack of sleep, praying (though I am not religious) for twenty more minutes of rest. Thirty minutes would be better. I roll over on my side because I can't get comfortable on my back and my breasts are too swollen to sleep on my stomach. Still not comfortable, I close my eyes anyway. Beggars can't be choosers.

I feel Sam's arm curve over my hip as he nestles into the space behind me. His hand strokes my belly—soft, warm and doughy, with a scar above my pubic area that is not as red and raw-looking as it was a few weeks ago—and I sigh in frustration. I just want to sleep.

I don't like him touching me. I don't like anyone touching me. My body is not my body, it hasn't been for months and months. First it belonged to the creature growing inside it, stretching it to maximum capacity. Now it belongs to the baby I birthed just nine weeks ago, the baby still sleeping in the next room the way I want to be sleeping right now. The baby who will be awake soon, screaming and wriggling and demanding. Latching on to breasts that don't produce enough milk to nourish him despite their size.

I try to remember if I made any bottles of formula before I fell into bed at 3 AM. I can't recall.

I want to squirm away as Sam moves his hand up to cup one tender breast, but there is nowhere for me to go, and besides, I'm too tired. Too tired to move, too tired to give him what he wants, too tired to think. Bone tired. No one ever told me I'd be this tired.

"Don't," I whisper, my voice barely audible for fear of waking the baby. "I'm tired."

"Me, too, sweetheart. Me, too," Sam says gently, though he doesn't stop touching me, doesn't move away.

His fingers pluck at my nipple—gently, because he knows they're sensitive and sore from being put into service several times a day. He loves my breasts and thinks they're beautiful. I loathe them because they're swollen and misshapen and riddled with stretch marks and are inadequate to feed my child. But his gentle touch stirs something inside me and my breast responds, sending a few drops of precious fluid over the tip.

I moan in frustration. He assumes it is arousal because he reaches further along my rounded body and inflicts the same gentle touch on my other nipple. There is no milk this time, this breast is dry and useless. But it still responds to his touch, the dark nipple tightening with excitement.

This time, my moan is one of pleasure.

He palms my breast, massages it gently before releasing it and slipping his hand down to my flabby belly, stroking the rolls that were once taut skin from the growing baby inside. I never had abs to admire, but at least they were there—muscles to pull in the flab. The muscles have been cut and no longer care to hold anything in. Between the scar and my belly button is a dead zone—I feel nothing there except that peculiar sensation of weight as if I'm leaning against something. The area is numb from the surgery and might always be, but I know his hand is there, running along the ridges of purple marks. "Badges of honor" my mother calls them. What does she know? She didn't have stretch marks with any of her four pregnancies.

Sam is still touching me, still not taking the hint that I just want to be left alone. I cringe in revulsion, wondering why I didn't slip on a T-shirt before I crawled into bed. The answer is simple, of course: after feeding the baby what little milk I had and supplementing with another two ounces of formula, I was too tired to put on a T-shirt. I was almost too tired to walk down the hall to the bedroom and might have curled up in the chair in the baby's room and gone to sleep if not for the fear that I might snore and wake the baby.

I have told him that I am the opposite of touch-deprived, that having a newborn has made me touch over-loaded. Even the gentlest of touches, a hug or backrub, feels like sharp nails on a fresh sunburn. I don't want to be touched, but some part of me still longs for the connection of touch. To know I am more than a mother, a sometimes milk maker, a Frankenstein's monster of stretch marks and skin discolorations and numb flesh and that ugly scar.

"Let me," he whispers, as if sensing the war going on inside me. The minutes are ticking away.

He slips his hand beneath the waistband of my panties and rests two fingers on my slit. He has not touched this part of me in over five months. Three months of pelvic rest followed by two months of postpartum recovery, recommended by my doctor despite the Cesarean delivery. That was something else they didn't tell me—that I would bleed for several weeks even if I didn't deliver the baby vaginally. The bleeding has long since stopped and I got the green light to resume sexual activity at my postpartum check-up, so we could have had sex by now, if I had wanted to. But I haven't.

He does not move his fingers, he just leaves them there, straddling my pussy lips. I am freshly shaven. Well, it's been two days but that's still fresh for me. I didn't shave in anticipation of having sex or because he prefers me that way, but because the hair that had grown back since the birth had been driving me crazy. I often awoke (when I was able to sleep) scratching myself. So out of practicality, I shaved. I'm all about practicality these days. It's called survival.

I may be tired, but my newly bare pussy is responding to the fingers touching it for the first time in five months. I have masturbated a few times since the bleeding stopped, always with my vibrator because it is the quickest (and therefore most practical) way, mostly to help me fall asleep (again with the practicality) and always when he was in the shower or feeding the baby. I didn't want him to think it was an invitation for him to do more. But now my pussy is issuing its own invitation, moistening under the weight of his still fingers, becoming swollen.

"Is this okay?" Sam asks, bringing his fingers together so that they press against my opening and my now-engorged clitoris.

What do I say? No? Stop? I don't want to have sex with you ever again? Let me sleep, goddamnit? All of the above?

I say what my pussy wants me to say. "It's okay. Yes, it's okay."

His touch remains slow, lazy, as if we have all the time in the world even though we don't. He dips his fingers into my pussy, gathers some moisture there and drags his fingertips over my clit. I shiver. Vibrators are lovely, efficient things, but they do not compare to the touch of someone who knows me and my body. The best part is, I don't have to do it for myself. I can lie there and let him get me off. If I were a good and selfless lover, I'd reach behind me and return the favor. Stroke his growing erection as it presses against my ass. But my days are spent being a selfless mother and I have nothing left to give him. So I am selfish. I let him touch me and I simply enjoy it.

"Yes," I whisper to my pillow. "More. Keep touching me."

Despite my exhaustion, my hips begin to move on their own. Finding a rhythm I thought my body had forgotten. He moans behind me, presses against me. I feel something like feminine pride blossoming the way my pussy is swelling and opening.

He moves his hand from my pussy to fumble between us. He is freeing his cock from his boxers. I debate what to do. I had hoped he would just get me off, give me a quick little orgasm so I could get fifteen, maybe twenty minutes of sleep. It crosses my mind that if I give him what he wants, maybe he'll get up and feed the baby and I could buy myself another hour. An hour!

This is what new parenthood has done to me. I consider bartering my body for more sleep. Me, who used to want to fuck all the time.

But then he's there, nestled in the crack of my ass, warm and hard and familiar and I'm wiggling again, even while I'm trying to figure out what I can get away with and squeeze out a few minutes of rest.

"Baby, you're driving me crazy," he murmurs, kissing my neck. His cheek is rough with stubble and his voice sounds as tired as I feel. This hasn't been easy for him either. But his body is still his body, he still looks the same, if a little more tired and disheveled. Nothing a shower and a shave and a cup of coffee won't cure, I can't even have coffee because I'm still trying to breastfeed.

I reach behind me and rub him. I'm startled by how strange it feels to touch him like this. We'd fucked like rabbits right up until I started spotting and my doctor said no more sex until after the baby came. That certainly put a damper on my sex drive. But here it was again, waking up even while I was feeling like I was swimming through a fog of exhaustion.

I angled my hips down and back, pressing my ass against him as I guided him to my entrance. I didn't have the energy to get on top of him and I didn't want him on top of me, compressing my belly—or worse, looking at me—but this, this I could do. I felt the head of his cock nudge between my swollen lips. He moaned when he felt the warm wetness inside, waiting for him.

"Oh, Carolyn, baby, you feel so good."

I whimpered in reply. He felt so good inside me, filling me as he slid into me slowly. The benefit of a Caesarean delivery was no pain in intercourse—no tender incision, no tearing, just blissful pleasure.

He gripped my hips and pulled me back on his cock until he was fully seated inside me. I let out a long, low moan. This—this—was what I'd been missing. Our position was awkward for more than slow, languid lovemaking, but I yearned for more.

"Harder," I whispered. "I want you harder."

He responded by lifting my leg and draping it over his hip. Holding onto my thigh for leverage, he began to fuck me with long, driving strokes. My breasts bounced against each other, my stomach jiggled in a comic way, my ass slapped noisily against his thighs and stomach with every stroke, but I didn't care. For the first time in months, I wasn't focused on any other part of my body except my pussy. And while the rest of me may have expanded and shifted in ways that might never return to normal or feel completely familiar, my pussy was wet and aroused and very, very much mine.

"Yes, yeah," I whimpered, slipping my hand down between my thighs to manipulate my clit while he fucked me. "Fuck me, Sam."

And he did. Where his touch had been gentle before, solicitous through pregnancy and postpartum recovery, non-sexual when helping me maneuver the baby to my breast, now he was rough, demanding, selfish. My skin tingled where he touched me, grabbed me, still gentle with my breasts, but firm with my hips, ass, shoulders, thighs. He pulled my leg higher and covered my hand with his own, both of us sliding our fingers along my wet slit, toying with my clit, stroking his cock as it slid in and out of me. Panting, sweaty, fucking like we hadn't fucked since—

The unmistakable sound of the baby waking up brought everything to a halt. Sam went still inside me and I bit back a cry of frustration as I strained to listen. The baby monitor next to the bed echoed the sounds from down the hall—a cry, followed by a whimper. Then… quiet snuffling sighs.

"Do you think…?"

"Shh," I said in response to Sam's question. I fondled my neglected clit, and pushed my ass back toward him. "Just fuck me. Fuck me before he's really awake."

Sam chuckled, but he didn't argue. As if resetting the hands on a clock, he resumed his hard, steady thrusts inside me. We were quieter now, more conscious of the baby who would awaken any minute, but the passion was no less. I bit my lip to keep from moaning as I rubbed my clit with frantic strokes, aching for the kind of release I hadn't enjoyed in forever.

Burying his head in the curve of my neck to muffle his own moans, Sam quickened his thrusts. He was close. So was I. I arched against him as the dual touch of our fingers and the sensation of his cock rubbing me just the right way brought my orgasm crashing over me. My pussy tightened around his girth and that was all it took for him to join me, both of us gasping and moaning as quietly as possible, riding out the powerful release we'd almost been denied. He squeezed my hand as it rested over my mound and I gasped, my clit sensitive and still throbbing.

He went still against me. The sun was fully up now, shining fully on the bed as wetness pooled under us. His. Mine. Ours. I whimpered as he slipped his cock free of my pussy, feeling empty and bereft. Though it had been months, my body had remembered that feeling and now, even though I was sated, it wanted more.

As if reading my mind, Sam squeezed my hand over my mound, sending a shiver up my spine as my pussy clenched in response. "Soon, baby," he said. "When Henry is sleeping through the night, we're going to be spending a lot of time in bed not sleeping."

The baby's soft snuffles became louder and turned into full-fledged wails. I sighed and started to get out of bed, feeling a twinge of pain between my thighs as my tender pussy protested. Sam clasped my wrist and pulled me back down, nuzzling his face against my breasts.

"I have to feed him," I said, my voice weary with exhaustion even while maternal need quickened my pulse.

"Stay in bed and rest for a while." Sam got out of bed and adjusted his boxers. "I'll feed him."

I laughed, thinking better of telling him about the mental conversation I'd had with myself before we had sex. "Thanks, honey." I pulled the quilt over me and tucked my hand under my cheek as he left our bedroom to take care of the baby.

That's how it began. Nothing had changed, really. And yet, everything had. I was myself again. Or, if not myself, my newly discovered self. My sexy, soft, fuckable, maternal self. I smiled and closed my eyes. It was going to be the best nap of my life.

bills and girls

SAMANTHA LUCE

Beyoncé has a song about girls running the world. I wish it were true. Sadly, I think it's bills that run the world. At least, they run the world in my house. Bills, and the dollar fifty extra per hour my wife makes for working the graveyard shift at the prison.

Time doesn't only fly when you're having fun. It also whizzes by when you're working nine to five and your partner works twelve hour shifts from six p.m. to six a.m. Mix overtime into that equation and the hyperactive four-year-old love of my life who recently started having a regular bout with nightmares, and the next thing you know you're washing dishes, wondering how the hell it's been over four months since you made love to your very hot wife.

I think most everyone, if asked, would agree that four sexless months is enough to drive anyone insane. So, imagine what four months, two weeks, and three and a half days were doing to me. Just yesterday I was so horny I actually contemplated getting a cheap thrill by leaning against the washer during the spin cycle. I might have given into the temptation if my daughter Tricia hadn't come bounding into the laundry room demanding to know where her Pooh Bear was.

Toddlers are more effective than cold showers when it comes to putting your libido in check. The thought of sex didn't cross my mind again until much later. In fact, it was actually at the very beginning of the next day. My teeny bladder, which had never quite recovered from childbirth, woke me around five a.m. As I relieved myself, I stared at the glass shower wall and the stone bench just inside the stall.

Four and a half months ago Dana had guided me onto that bench. Despite the steam, the wet stone remained cold. I squealed in surprise, about to object to the chill, when Dana's hands settled on my knees. Her big blue eyes locked onto mine. A mischievous smile quirked her full lips for just a moment before her hot mouth crashed into mine.

I spread my legs for her. She filled the void quickly, never breaking the kiss. Our breasts slid against each other's. The shower's wetness mixed with my own so that her fingers traveled over and inside my body with ease.

The buzz of a silenced text message broke me from my thoughts. I washed my hands and splashed some water on the heated skin of my face and the back of my neck before I made it to the bedside table to check my phone.

Dana's words filled the screen. "Hope I didn't wake you, Sexy. I can't get you out of my head. It's dead here. I miss you. I hope you see this when you wake up later and it makes you smile. Ciao Bella."

I chuckled softly. If she only knew. Everything about her makes me smile. She's the beautiful one. Just one look at the chin length auburn hair that perfectly frames her high cheekbones and the bright periwinkle eyes surrounded by thick, dark lashes makes me weak. Seven years have not dulled the flame I carry in my heart for her.

The shower caught my attention again. A sleep- and sex-deprived scheme was mucking around in my head. I held off on the shower just long enough to strip the bed and make it again with fresh sheets and a comforter. I shifted the pillows to make it look like I was under the covers. Dana never turns on the lights when she enters our room early in the morning. She's always quiet and makes a beeline for the shower. The fluffed pillows should be enough to fool her.

I tiptoed down the hall to Tricia's room. The soft pink glow of her nightlight highlighted the peaceful smile on her face. From the looks of it, the nightmares had been kept at bay by something much more enjoyable. I blew her a kiss and said a silent prayer of gratitude before heading back to my room.

I checked the clock after I showered. I had only a handful of minutes to spare. I turned off the lights and hid behind the bathroom door. My breaths were quick and shallow. What I was doing was crazy. I could barely stifle the urge to laugh at my half-baked plan to ravage my wife.

Right before I chickened out, the bathroom door eased open. I watched her in silhouette as she removed the heavy utility belt and hung it inside the custom cabinet above the toilet. Before she could turn around, I slid my arms around her waist.

She grabbed my arm and spun me away from her. Next thing I knew, I was face first against the bathroom door with my arm twisted painfully behind me. "Babe, it's me," I gasped before she applied more pressure.

"Holy shit, Erin." She quickly let me go and fumbled for the light switch. "Are you crazy? Sneaking up on a correctional officer is never a good plan." She stepped closer behind me and started massaging the shoulder she'd just twisted. Her lips brushed against my ear and she kissed me softly. "What in the world were you thinking?" Her whispered words brought goosebumps to my neck.

"I don't know." I shrugged. "Clearly I wasn't thinking. I-I just woke up starving for you and I missed you. A lot."

"I missed you too," She kissed my ear again. "And I'm so sorry I hurt you. Are you okay?"

I nodded and sheepishly turned around to face her, suddenly very self-conscious of my nudity and the few extra pounds that I couldn't shake since giving birth to Tricia. The ones Dana insists aren't there. "Glad you didn't go with a full body slam."

She laughed. "Thank God it's too tight to perform that move in here. Are you sure you're okay?"

"My pride hurts a little, but I'll live."

"Your pride should be up about a hundred notches. You're beautiful. I was dead tired until I got a look at you in the buff. I still can't wait to get into bed," She winked and flashed my favorite smirk. "But there's a new list of things I want to do in that bed with you, and sleep is nowhere on the list."

I took her hand and pulled her closer. Watching her watching me, a moan escaped my lips.

"Don't tease me. It's late." She shook her head. She looked genuinely conflicted. "No, I mean it's early for you. You should be sleeping."

"No teasing," I agreed, brushing my lips against the corner of her mouth. "No sleeping." I kissed her again. My free hand tugged at the tie around her neck. "No clothes either." I gently nudged her backward. "Strip."

"Seriously?"

I slid onto the counter, letting my legs inch slowly apart. The moment I had her attention where I wanted it, I softly cleared my throat. Her eyes slowly trailed the length of my body until she caught sight of me sucking two fingers. Her breath caught. I gave one last lick before lowering my hand between my legs. "Take it all off for me, baby."

Her hands flew to her shirt buttons in a frenzy.

"Slow down." I gradually slipped my fingers inside. "Don't go so fast."

"You're killing me," she whispered. The speed of her movements reduced by only a hair. Before all the buttons were undone, she pulled the shirt and tie over her head and tossed them to the floor. The bra came next. Nipples as stiff and tasty as a perfect meringue sprang into view. It might have been going on five months, but I'd never forget the flavor of her smooth skin.

I heard a whimper followed immediately by quiet laughter from Dana and I realized in mock horror the whimper had come from me.

"Am I turning you on?" She was grinning when she loosened the snap on her pants and undid the zipper.

Swallowing a lump of desire, I raised my very wet fingers to show her. "What do you think, love?"

She caught my wrist and brought the fingers to her lips. After a deep inhale, she slowly sucked the digits into her warm mouth.

I slid my other hand to her waist and freed her from her pants and briefs. She pulled me from the counter and I wrapped my legs tightly around her hips. Her strength and balance kept us both upright as she reached to turn the shower on.

Steam quickly fogged the glass doors. It took some coaxing to convince Dana to set me down inside the stall. I backed away to get a better look as the water sluiced over her toned body. The view stole my breath. If I kept looking at the front of her glorious form I knew I'd lose every bit of self-control I had. I summoned strength from somewhere and turned her away from me.

Her hands left their marks on the glass when I pressed her against it. I picked up her favorite vanilla and sandalwood body wash and took my time lathering her from head to toe while she worked the shampoo through her locks.

She gave me a moment to admire her suds-covered body before she stepped under the heavy spray. I snatched the second nozzle from the wall and used it to rinse the areas I wanted to taste the most.

When she nudged me toward the bench, I did a quick sidestep and eased her down onto the cement. She'd worked all night. I couldn't bear to see her stand for another minute. I sat beside her and kissed her deeply. My fingers mapped paths to all her favorite spots and mine.

She was panting when my mouth began to follow all the paths. "Holy shit, what's gotten into you?"

"I got your text." I stepped off the bench and lowered myself between her knees. "I missed you too." I trailed kisses up and down between her knees and thighs, marveling at her trembling muscles. The pads of my fingers tickled her legs to get her to open even wider. My lips were just millimeters from her mound. "Doesn't it feel like it's been forever since I made you come?"

She groaned and arched herself off the bench. My mouth locked onto her as my hands went round to give her some support.

Her strong fingers worked their way through my hair, cradling me with her hand and grinding herself against me at the same time. Her tangy ambrosia drew my tongue deeper inside until she had nothing more to give.

When my own legs stopped quivering and I could raise myself

to sit beside her on the bench, I gave her a long, slow kiss. She pressed against me and her hot, wet skin slid all over mine until we both collapsed to opposite corners of the bench.

The bills don't get to run the world today. On this day, Beyoncé got it mostly right. Not just girls, but moms, run the world.

the treadmill

BRANDY FOX

I need exercise like I need air and food and sex. If I go a day without a good hard workout at the gym, or at least a run around the neighborhood, I get so grumpy my kids call me *Mommy From The Black Lagoon.* I growl at Sean when he playfully grabs my ass or reels me in for a kiss. I sulk and whine until the kids hide in their rooms and Sean literally pushes me out the door, tossing my running shoes onto the front porch and locking the deadbolt.

This morning is no different. It's been more than 24 hours since my last workout. Sean has to save the kids from my wrath and hustle them out the door to catch their bus. A torrential rain forces me to drive to the gym. I walk past the front counter and inhale the smell of sweat and lemon-scented cleaner— aromatherapy for workoutaholics. Instantly, my body sighs.

As usual, I choose a treadmill near the wall of windows. I want nothing in front of me but tree-covered hills speckled with suburban homes. I plug into a music mix and start the machine at 3.0 to warm-up for a long run. Already my bad mood is fading, replaced by guilt about my behavior that morning. Details I normally don't miss come flooding in: Did I actually get the lunches in the kids' backpacks? Did I remind Jenna to meet me after school for her piano lesson instead of taking the bus home? Crap. I didn't sign Evan's Friday folder. Nor did I remember to take ground beef out of the freezer for dinner tonight.

I punch it up to 4.0 and start jogging. My feet hit a stride in time with *Girls Just Wanna Have Fun*. At last my mind lets go of the guilt and wanders through other, more interesting thoughts. Like how the rain is streaking the windows like sweat on a bare back. And how when I arrived there were two men on treadmills behind me. Are they admiring my glutes as they flex and stretch in a steady rhythm?

I take it to 5.0 and run. My breath quickens. A bead of perspiration slides down the small of my back. It's feeling moist back there. Is there a wet spot on my spandex? I keep thinking about the men behind me, their eyes caressing my chiseled shoulders and long neck. I notice my G-string catching my labia and suddenly my entire body is focused on that rhythmic catch-release, catch-release, again and again as my legs swing across the treadmill belt. I check my heart rate monitor and notice it's jumped up by 20. Hear my heavy breathing despite the earphones and Nelly singing, *It's gettin' hot in here, so take off all your clothes.*

Wait, was I just singing out loud?!

My entire body is humming now. Calm down, for god's sake! Save it for Date Night with Sean tomorrow.

Great. Now I'm thinking about Date Night. Anticipating the goodbyes as the kids set off for the neighbor's house while Sean makes the vodka tonics. Then slipping between the sheets, relishing the quiet and nursing our drinks like we have all evening, because we do.

Our conversation always starts with the family—our weekly managerial meeting—then wanders to household decisions, our careers and various volunteer jobs, then finally to us. To admiring a taut bicep or teasing about a new gray hair or wrinkle. To legs tangling under the sheets, lips finding ears, fingers fondling hair and hips and nipples and ohhh…

I look around the gym. Everyone is in their own little workout world, plugged into their music or conversation while pumping their Stairmasters and ellipticals and stationary bikes. I focus on the windows—the swaying trees, the driving rain, the hills like a curvy woman—and there it is, that tantalizing catch-release, catch-release of my labia, so close to my clit. If I press my thighs together just a little…Oh there! Oh my…

It's that delicious moment when Sean's mouth moves down the length of my body to taste my clavicle and breasts and belly that all of me opens wide in welcome and I'm giddy with anticipation. At last it all goes away—the daily grind of work and school and soccer practice and piano lessons and homework—just slips off the bed and out the door. My mind frees itself from the To Do list and the Family Calendar and rests on a soft pillow of utter pleasure.

Catch-release, catch-release—each cycle now sends a jolt of electricity through my groin. My chest is heaving and I pause the music to see what others might hear coming from my corner of the gym. A woman running hard. A woman at the peak of her workout. I look at my reflection in the window. They might see lines of sweat trailing down my cleavage and into my sports bra, a dark spot over my pubic bone, a slack jaw and open mouth gulping for oxygen.

I swallow the moans that on Date Night would be coming fast now as Sean flips me onto my stomach, fingers my slit and presses his cock into the small of my back. I get to my knees and lean against his firm chest, let the wiry hair there tickle my back as his mouth wanders down my neck and across my shoulder. One hand cups and pinches my breasts while the other presses against my mound and fondles my clit. I find the lube, squeeze a blob on my palm and reach behind. When my cold hand slides up his firm rod, he quivers.

I am bare to the windows and trees and hills. At least that's what I imagine now at 6.0, running so fast I'm panting. I can't slow down or I'll fall of the treadmill. Can't stop and oh, it's so slick down there that the string is wedging its way deeper into my folds, pressing and pulling my labia and anus so that they're two nodes, a current zapping back and forth between them. The fabric of my sports bra rubs against my nipples. Add to that my quick breaths and there's a symphony playing inside my body, yet invisible and silent to everyone else.

Or is it? Do the men behind me see my wet crotch and wonder? Can they hear my heavy breathing and sense my arousal? What would they think if they knew what this middle-aged soccer mom was really up to?

When Sean enters me slow and slick, I gasp. After twenty years, I still gasp every time, because being filled up with a man as devoted as him is breathtaking. I brace myself on the bed frame and rock my pelvis slowly. We give so much attention to everything else in our lives, let's give this some time, too. This… oh yeah… this totally utterly completely self-indulgent act that pleasures only us, honors what we made together, what we've created with this, this… ohhh… this sacred rite.

Twenty years ago, I was embarrassed to touch myself in front of Sean, but now, oh boy… my own fingers massage my nub with abandon. Every thrust, sometimes slow and sometimes fast, is aimed at that spot of pure bliss deep inside me. I squeeze my thighs and Kegel in a dance we've perfected. And it never. Ever. Gets. Old.

At last the current ignites, blasting from my groin to my stomach and down my legs. I step off the treadmill just as my knees buckle and brace my body against the machine's armrests. I can't help but gasp openly as spasms ripple through my ass. When they finally pass, I lay my head in my hand to hide the smile stretching my flushed cheeks. I'd be just another woman pushing herself too hard on the treadmill if it weren't for my hysterical giggling.

When I finally get myself under control, I straighten up and towel off my chest and underarms. Then I dare to look around. The two men who were behind me are gone. Everyone is still in their own workout worlds except for a woman whose eyes bounce from the TV screen to me, like she can't help looking.

Is it my imagination, or do her eyes twinkle with knowing?

tocks in my ticker

POOJA PANDE

The clock is ticking.

I never really understood—or cared to understand—the biological clock. Sameer and I had Rasik "late", as they say in Sameer's family. And mine. And all of India's, for that matter. We like to have our kids "early"—preferably in the first two years of marriage. I always find myself explaining this to my expat friends and my American sister-in-law, but if you've had a child by the time your first wedding anniversary is around the corner, or just past, you're like the "It" couple, as far as your relatives are concerned. My mum even came up with a logical argument to support this: "It's best to have it out of the way as soon as possible, so it's done." But Sameer and I chose not to fall into that trap, taking our own sweet time. Rasik, our little boy who's turning five in another month and is the joy of our lives, came into our lives after a good five years of being married.

But while that clock was a trap, this actual one—the one that showed me the time and was now clocking at midnight, inching its way forward, slowly and very surely toward one in the morning when, inevitably, Rasik would charge into our bedroom, Mickey Mouse duvet trailing behind him—this clock was only too real.

And it was ticking.

I thought five years of marriage had taught me everything there was to learn and know about sex. Sameer and I had discovered (and duly noted) our likes and dislikes in the bedroom. There were several happy encounters along the way; a few accidents, even, like the time he swished his whisky a little too jerkily and the ice plonked right into my cleavage and down my top and I loved it, it soon became my thing. Some had transpired willfully, but urged on by external sources, like the time we saw that Hollywood movie together and tried the wheelbarrow. That one made me embrace yoga with a vengeance. And we'd definitely tried stuff neither of us had liked. That whole pour-Hershey's-all-over-your-partner-and- lick-it-off-routine that they'll have you believe is the hottest thing ever, is actually just plain messy. You fantasize about a bath the whole time.

Most of our activities had been declarations of the body, by the body, for the body, to rephrase the constitutional dictum. The body has its way of establishing superiority over and above anything else, especially when there's another body in such close proximity, both willing and able.

I had successfully coaxed Sameer to move out of his parents' house even before we'd celebrated our first anniversary. With just the two of us under one roof and the entire expanse of the night to explore between the two of us, there wasn't much we hadn't tried. The night was long, the night was young, and we owned that moon.

But when Rasik came along, things changed. Nights became about feeding, burping, cleaning, soothing, crying spells (grown-ups and baby), tantrums, changing diapers, heating the formula, and then if you were lucky, some sleeping. That first year, we were both going a little mad and often at each other, and unlike times before, we could never find the time or the mind space to resolve it in bed. "There's no argument that can't be solved between the sheets," my aunt had said to me—mysteriously, then—when I had proclaimed to her, as a feisty teenager, that I wasn't going to marry anyone because I'd just be fighting with him all day. Words of wisdom, I realized, each time Sameer and I fought. But now we were all fight no fuck, and it was telling on us.

Another whirlwind year or two and we took the most un-Indian decision to move Rasik out of our bedroom and into his own. Sameer's mom judged me from Chandigarh, which is where they'd moved to since they didn't want to see me too often, and even my own colleagues at work tut-tutted behind my back, I knew. I'd once walked into a lunch session I wasn't expected at, and one of the junior executives had held her tongue mid-sentence, but it was too late. "The poor baby has to live with the nanny all day while she's here and then even at night, she doesn't want to have anything to do with him. Making him sleep in another room. What a mother, imagine!" It had tortured me for weeks. How much, I wondered, must we mothers do before someone decides it's enough? That it's time for mothers to be happy?

It's a year-plus now and we're in the final transition phase where Rasik sleeps on his bed, in his own room, for four or five hours straight before sauntering into ours when he semi-wakes up. He plonks right in the middle of his parents and goes back to the deep sleep he'd barely come out of two seconds before.

It's a *big* deal; it had started with less than 20 minutes. We'd put him to bed and tiptoe out and he'd jump right out, like a jack in the box. Some nights, we'd just about started kissing when we'd hear the familiar thump that was Rasik getting out of bed and we'd have to promptly stop before we'd even "got our freak on" as Sameer sometimes liked to say. One night, I had my hand inside Sameer's pants even as he was unhooking my bra when Rasik ran in. We were both petrified for weeks after, certain that we'd scarred him for life, and living in constant fear of what he might say at school, what he saw his mommy and daddy do. I was living in terror the whole week, expecting the phone to ring with his teacher wanting a word with the irresponsible parents about "what Rasik told us during circle time when they're sharing stories about home".

But the last few months have been miraculous because Sameer and I, we've got our nights back. At least, some of them. I feel like I've clawed my way back into my past, all need and sweat and lust, with an enhanced appreciation for the quickie.

See, that ticking clock demands an urgency. I am a slave to that moving hand. Sameer and I both, enslaved by Time, our ball-and-chain routine. My body now times itself to the ticks and the tocks. Some nights when I read Rasik his bedtime book, Dr. Seuss gets shaded dirty hues in my dirty mind. Like Mr. and Mrs. J. Carmichael Krox, I know that I've got ticks in my tocker and Sameer, tocks in his ticker. And I know that the reading of this book is the last PG-13 thing I'll be doing that night. My naked body will soon be entwined in Sameer's, bathed in moonlight streaming in through our sheer curtains that we decided to put up in the bedroom on a whim, but also because we live on the 15th floor and nobody is watching. Sometimes when Sameer's traveling on work, he calls me from his hotel room and whispers over the phone to me, telling me how the moonlight is reminding him of me and an involuntary shudder goes through my body. It's a miracle how the body tunes itself to new rhythms. Earlier, when Time was on our side, we would take our time with everything. I would do a striptease *slowly* if that's the kind of mood we were in, or Sameer would flip out his phone and make a video of our foreplay—hours of footage of us just pleasuring each other. He would linger on my erect nipples, finger my clit; I would mount him and move ever so *slowly* and then take him in my mouth. And then we'd go again. We would spend hours this way before any actual penetration. There were nights we wouldn't sleep at all, and then sleep in the twilight zone—the *nap* was the quickie. Two to five in the morning. We'd sleep like babies then, happy, contented, naked.

But now the clock, it ticks. Sensing the onset of the Rasik hour, I feel a surge in my chest and that butterfly-flutter in my stomach that spells anticipation. My body seeks out Sameer, almost Pavlovian, whether he's huddled over his laptop, poring over excel spreadsheets or streaming the latest Silicon Valley episode, and it always wins. On some nights, Sameer jumps me in the hallway even before Time has spelled out its plans, and impatient, we start ripping each other's clothes off.

Tonight, Rasik has slept lightly, we know it. One ear cocked towards the sound of any light thumps from the adjacent room, speed is of the ultimate essence yet again, and it propels us on, urges us to hasten. And the more we hasten, the hotter it gets. When Sameer slows down the thrusting waiting for me, I push aside his generosity and moan into his ear, commanding him to bite the side of my neck, willing my own body to get with the program. The absolute disrespect for slowing anything down excites Sameer and very soon, he's figured out how to nibble on my breasts while pushing inside me even as I tighten myself around his throbbing cock, the ripples already beginning to form.

We transform into masters of the artful quickie tonight. There is something deliciously gratifying in this—this knowledge; knowing that we could do this together. Not just meet or find or stumble upon bliss, but grab it, demand it, take it by the cock and the clit and ask it to relent, to surrender, to come.

Tomorrow, when the girls at the office indulge in those bitch-fests they call smoke breaks and get their kicks maligning my maternal prowess, and when those boring relatives judge me for abandoning Rasik at night—the same relatives who judged me before for not having him "early"—I know it won't get to me. I'll be getting by thinking of impending bedtimes; a loving story with the baby, and a story of loving to follow, with my baby.

I know I'll look at my watch as the workday draws to its end, just as I stare at the clock now in our bedroom—pride of place it has on the wall—as Sameer and I climax seconds apart and I hold him in after, like I always do.

He glances at it too.

Because yes, the clock, it's ticking.

mom's night out

J.A. REED

I thought life was supposed to get easy as I got older.

That's not to say that I don't enjoy or like my life. I wouldn't trade it in for the world. I love my two kids (though they would probably hate to hear me call them kids in their teenage years). I love my husband and our life together. And I love my job teaching young minds the classics of literature that have withstood the test of time. It's a satisfying life.

But it's a pain in the ass sometimes.

I love my rewarding career as an English teacher. As clichéd as it might sound, I do think I make a difference in the lives of some of my students, past and present. I love my students, and I love being able to introduce timeless classics to them, foster discussions, and open their minds. But after fourteen years of teaching the same curriculum year in and year out, having to read dull and dry essays by students who clearly wished to be doing better things with their time, grappling with education politics and parents, it becomes tiresome.

Where to begin at home? Those two children of mine never fail to test their boundaries and try to establish new avenues of freedom in their lives. They're at that time when they're finding their voice, searching for their independence, challenging me along the way. And my husband... He does provide a good, stable life for his family. He's been a supportive and caring husband, always there to lend an ear when I prattle on about department meetings or asinine parent-teacher conferences. But while he's there emotionally, he's not always there physically.

It wasn't always the case, but after a while, David and I just naturally found each other drifting further and further apart. Our careers were consuming, our kids only strained it more. Our little intimate moments became fewer and fewer, dissolving away into something that seemed obligatory, a chore and duty to one another before going back to our busy routines.

Sometimes, I just needed to take a break.

It's something I do once a year, when I just need to get away. The stresses of my career as a teacher, and the headaches that come with raising two teenagers on my own while my husband works long hours, just creates that deep need within to just shut down and take a break. Get away and unwind. Unplug myself. Do something I *want* to do for a change. I have always felt lucky that David understands and accepts it, and doesn't try to inject himself into my little time to myself.

My routine varies. Sometimes, it's a trip to the spa, exiting relaxed and refreshed. Or some nights, when I just need to get away, it might just be a night at the mall and movies all by myself, unencumbered by the desires or demands of my family or friends, going to the shops I want to go into, seeing the films I want to see, having only myself to shop for and please. Sometimes I check myself into a hotel downtown for the night.

I would splurge a bit on myself. A room at one of the nicer hotels in the city. A bed with soft, satin sheets. Windows that gave an impressive view of the sprawling metropolis below.

I didn't usually intend on spending the night holed up in my room. But sometimes I did, with room service and trashy reality television. In recent years, I had been wanting something else: reassurance.

It was something that had been missing in my personal life. I thought I looked good. I still tried to keep myself in shape. During the summer, I would spend my days active, rather than parking it inside like so many of my colleagues did during the long summer months. I watched what I ate and drank, and exercised almost daily. But while I might have felt like I looked good, hearing it was something that had been absent in my life. David sometimes complimented me, but the way he said it—so often fatigued from work—sounded almost like an automatic, canned response.

Those nights of escape began to take on a whole new meaning. They became the moments when I could see if I still had "it" in my early forties. I'd venture out, going to bars and lounges, just to drink and be looked at, talked to and flirted with. Nothing more, nothing less. All I wanted was that validation, that confirmation in myself and my confidence.

On my most recent night out, I arrived at the Ambassador downtown late in the afternoon, my lone bag in hand. After a long, relaxing soak and scrub in the bathtub, I found myself down in the hotel lounge by eight, feeling comfortable and fitting in with the business crowd that had apparently gathered for after-work drinks. With a drink in hand, I sat alone at the bar, taking in the sights and sounds around me.

A part of me wondered who, if anyone, would be the first to approach the lonely lady at the bar. Sometimes I didn't have to wait long at all until some form of interest was shown. A conversation started up, a wink or nod, a free drink. Sometimes, I would have to wait a little, bide my time in the changing of crowds or bars. But on that night, I worried that might not happen at all, with the younger-looking crowd, and assortment of women half my age. I felt self-conscious, as I always did, in those stretches of time, sitting dressed up, having felt so confident before I left my hotel room, only to find myself alone, surrounded by the younger, prettier women who were so often more desirable.

Was it fate? A stroke of ill luck on that night? Was it me? I would ask myself such questions over and over again as I sat alone. Would that be the year my confidence came crumbling down? It was an agonizing wait, full of self-doubt and gloom.

I was ready to call it an early night. I was ready to finish my whiskey and make the long walk up to my room, where I was planning to drown my thoughts with a bottle of wine.

"Excuse me, Mrs. Allen?" A man's voice asked from behind me. "Mrs. Betty Allen?"

My ears perked at the voice, and my mind filled with a certain, sudden unease. When I went out, when I treated myself, I never used my actual name outside of the necessity when checking in to the hotel. That was a part of the appeal of going out on my nights. I wasn't Betty Allen, English teacher at Jefferson High. I wasn't Betty Allen, mother and wife. I was whoever I wanted to be. A mystery that I could lose myself within, a character from a story, just for the night.

I turned around, swiveling on my bar stool with a look of warmth that was congenial. My mind raced with the various possibilities of who found me. But the man who met my gaze looked like a complete stranger, failing to register in my memory.

Whomever he was, he made an immediate impact in my mind. Tall, at least six feet, and young. He was clean shaven, with short, neat hair cropped close to his scalp. The chiseled, strong jaw was matched by a firm, athletic body beneath the plain suit he wore.

"Yes?" I asked, slightly confused as my mind still tried to figure out who would know me.

He laughed in a gentle way, a soft chuckle. "I suppose you don't remember me." His hands were tucked in his pockets as he gave a slight shrug. "James Parker. You used to teach—"

"James?" I interrupted in an incredulous way. "James Parker?"

Every few years, a teacher was blessed to have a special student. One who was bright, intelligent, who was actually interested in the subject. The displaying of such interest, such potential, could so often brighten a teacher's day. Students like that made teaching worthwhile.

James was a bright young man. Awkward and shy. It could be like pulling teeth to get him involved and engaged in discussions. He preferred to remain quiet in the back of the classroom. But his writing... I still keep his submissions to pass around my classes, using his work as an example of how a paper should be written. He would come by after school sometimes, just to talk and discuss whatever book we were currently reading in class, his views always so thoughtful and engaging.

He was a far cry from the man who stood before me, with that charm, that smirk upon his face as he nodded his head.

The James I knew had been an awkward young man. A skinny, lanky, bespectacled youth with untamed hair. A young man who did not strike me as becoming the bar type, but rather someone who would prefer to stay home with their books or computers. He wasn't this handsome, attractive man. And yet... Just when the thought of it being some sort of wild ruse, the look in his eyes, that familiar brown hue, looked back.

"Yeah. It's me." He said with a slight, awkward laugh. "I grew up a bit."

I couldn't help a short laugh escape my lips in that moment. "I'll say."

His chuckle made my cheeks redden. "Well, you still look the same as ever."

The color in my cheeks deepened. The same? I tried to do the math. Seven years? I felt a surge of pride and confidence that I hadn't felt in some time.

It felt awkward to be sitting there, complimenting and being complimented upon looks. In a way, my mind still thought of him as that shy, reserved young student in my class. It was hard to reconcile the handsome, strong-looking man that stood before me with the young man I had taught Shakespeare to all those years ago.

"I saw you from across the room." He nodded towards a small group of younger individuals talking among themselves. "I couldn't resist a chance to come over and say hello."

"Well I'm glad you did." I said. "I was just about to pay my bill."

A look of mild surprise came from him. "Oh. I figured you were waiting for your husband."

The words should have made me feel ashamed. To hear the words from his lips, the knowledge that I was out on the town, alone by myself on a Friday night in a bar, while my husband was at home. It should have made me feel awkward. But from James, there was no accusatory spice in his voice. Nothing but a curious observation.

I smiled at his words. "No. It's just me tonight. It's my annual Night Out."

"Annual night out, huh?" He asked. "Sounds entertaining. May I?"

Before I could even contemplate a denial out of decorum, my former student slid in beside me and took the unoccupied bar stool to my right. For a moment, I was treated to an appealing scent on him, one that was uniquely masculine and clean, a hint of aftershave. It was unlike anything my husband possessed in his limited collection.

I scrambled for a moment to come up with something to say as he ordered a whiskey like myself. "So how have you been?" I finally asked. "It's been ages."

"I guess it has." He laughed gently. "I can remember being back in your class like it was yesterday."

My snort of amusement came to pass before he continued.

"I've been doing well, I guess. I went to college, learned a lot about myself, about life, and a whole bunch of other bullshit." He grinned slyly. . "I got into publishing, because of this awesome teacher in high school."

What blood that had begun to recede from my cheeks came flooding back.

We talked for a while there, at the bar in the hotel lounge. Tales of how we were doing, what we were doing, and the like were traded back and forth. How he had started as a proofreader, and worked his way up to editor. How I was still teaching English in my same classroom. We talked of books, of our latest literary conquests. We talked of what was going on in our lives.

Sitting there with him was a breath of fresh air, one that I had not anticipated. It was different than talking with my current students, where it was always sterile, in a sense. Professional and removed from deeper levels of personality. Talking with him felt different than even with some of my friends and colleagues. James was fresh and engaging, and he didn't drag on about disappointments in his personal and professional life.

And while we sat there together, I could not help but take note of the looks leveled our way. From more than a few of the younger women around the lounge in my field of view, I couldn't miss the occasional sense of jealousy, the look of curious interest as I sat next to and talked, so intimately, with one of the most attractive men in the whole room.

I felt a certain sense of pride in seeing those looks of jealousy. My grins in those moments could not be contained. In an age where younger always seemed better, when women of a certain age were so often looked to with little interest, it felt empowering in a way I had never felt in my nights out.

And I couldn't help feeling good about my unexpected guest sitting beside me.

I knew he was flirting with me here and there. I did not miss the little jokes and innuendo in our conversation. I too engaged in it a bit. I also did not fail to notice the way his eyes would occasionally glance down to the neckline of my dress.

I could have stopped him whenever I wanted. I could have put a halt to it easily, and I knew the respectable, courteous James Parker would have obliged. I could have put on my cardigan, feigning a slight chill. But I didn't.

It could have been blamed on the alcohol. But it was more than that. James Parker knew me. He knew that I was a mother of two teens, a married woman who taught high school English. There was no pretending to be someone else. I didn't have to wear a mask of anonymity or some made up story. James Parker was interested in me. James Parker was attracted to me.

It made me feel sexier than I ever could remember.

I should have seen what was coming. I should have politely declined his offer to walk me up to my room when I admitted that I was staying in the hotel. It would have been the right thing to do, for him, for my kids, my husband. It would have been the right thing, but I was buzzing from the alcohol and unexpected attention given to me on that magical night.

Cheating never seriously crossed my mind. But I would be lying if I didn't fantasize about the handsome young man who walked with me, arms linked, through the bar and to the bank of elevators in the lobby.

A light silence had fallen between us as we stood in the elevator. My eyes tried their best to avoid the appealing reflection of him in the mirror before us, trying instead to focus on the ticker above the door as the compartment rose through the building.

"You know," he said, breaking the silence. "I'm going to regret admitting this, but I've always had a crush on you."

My head turned towards him, looking up into those deep, entrancing eyes. I could feel my heartbeat rising, the voice in my head warning me to be calm and level-headed. I couldn't help but notice, however, that he spoke of always having a crush, not in the past tense.

I waved it off dismissively. "Yeah right."

"It's true." He said lightheartedly, but not having lost an edge of seriousness. "I mean, for years, I've thought about you. And tonight? Hands down, the sexiest woman there." James paused, his words sinking into my mind. "Your husband is a lucky guy."

The mention of David brought a derisive snort from me. In the short time of the reunion between James and me, he had shown me more interest than David had in weeks. When was the last time he looked at me in a way like James was at that moment? That look of carnal hunger, that confident lust?

It was on my mind as we departed the elevator and walked down the hall to my room. This young man, this strong, attractive, hunk of a man wanted me. He didn't care that I was married. He didn't care that I was a mother. He didn't care that I was a teacher into her forties. He could have chosen any of the young women down in the lounge.

And he wanted me.

He wanted to fuck me.

It was in his eyes as he looked at me when we came to a stop at my room door. The way he leaned against the wall, those beautiful eyes so full of lust, of hunger. For a moment, all I could do was look into those eyes, losing myself in all sorts of sordid, carnal thoughts. Him, on top of me. Me, on top of him. Our limbs entangled in hot, passionate bliss. My clitoris throbbed approvingly at the thought, my panties moistened from the damp heat of my sex. I wanted him desperately.

"Well, here we are." My fingers nervously toyed with the card in my hand. Say goodnight, I told myself. Say goodnight and go to bed. How easy it sounded.

"Here we are..." He acknowledged. "I had a great night."

"So did I."

"I'd love to talk again sometime, if that's all right with you."

I nodded my head. But my mind was on other things at that moment, lingering beyond the tantalizing images that danced through my mind. "Did you mean what you said?" I asked, unable to look at him. "Back in the elevator. Did you mean it?"

James straightened in his place. "I meant everything I said."

Words and looks alone had been enough in the past to give me that reassurance I sought in my later years. They sustained me, put the doubts and questions to rest. I was satisfied with them in the past. I could blame it on the alcohol, the stressful rigors of my career and life at home. But on that night, I wanted him. I wanted him more than anyone else.

I acted on impulse, following my heart. To wait any longer, to speak, would have only made the voice of my conscience stronger. I didn't think when I reached out and pulled at his tie. Not when I pulled his head down and pressed my lips against his. No thinking. Just acting.

The surprise caught him off guard. For a moment, he did not seem to know what to say or do. But soon he too acted accordingly, kissing back. I found myself pressed against my hotel door, his hard, firm body against mine, hands exploring one another through our clothes.

A sound of a door opening down the hall made us stop. Quickly we separated, looking flushed, hungry for more as a couple emerged from their room. With trembling legs and shaky fingers, I opened my door as quickly as I could before the nerve was lost. James didn't need any encouragement. He followed, closing the door behind him.

Our clothes came off in a blur. A mad dash to continue came over us like an anxious fervor. We had to be naked. We had to continue before reality set in. My dress came off, pulled over my head as he yanked away his tie and did away with his coat. The buttons of his shirt were unfastened, revealing a tight, strong body that made me groan. A far cry from the growing paunch of my husband.

As I unhooked my bra, he went to remove his pants. His slacks were unfastened along with his belt, shoved down his strong, thick thighs to reveal his rigid organ. It seemed as painfully hard as my pussy felt empty. That cock, so firm, so darkened with lust, was for me.

James smirked as he crossed the space between us, my eyes taking in the sight of him.

We didn't bother with foreplay. There was no sucking, no licking. Such detours would have only delayed what we both wanted then and there.

I lay beneath him, between the softness of the comforter and the hardness of his muscled form. Those thick, strong arms of his were planted on either side of my head, my eyes treated to the sight of his chiseled muscles as his cock pressed near my entrance.

It throbbed against me, so hot and heated, aching just as much as my clitoris was at that moment.

When he slid his thick, hardened cock inside of my wetness, it took my breath away. My hands found his back, gripping onto him as he pressed deeper into the tight canal that greeted him enthusiastically with the evidence of my arousal.

What began as slow, methodical probes of his hips soon gave way to a deeper intensity. Each thrust of his member carved away at my folds, stretching and filling me to a new level of satisfaction. He made me more aroused than any other man before, my husband a poor comparison to this young Adonis above and within me.

I felt so good, so full. Desired more than I ever had felt in my life. It was in those eyes, those intense eyes looking down into mine, that I lost myself to my first orgasm of the night.

I lost count of the number of times I came with him lodged so snug inside of me. For the first time in so long, I felt comfortable riding a man in the throes of passion, to feel his eyes looking up as we ground and fucked the night away. A look of pure desire, pure hunger. The passion, the heat, that had been lost in my marital bed had been found in the embrace and eyes of this man.

In those moments, I should have felt a chilling sense of shame. Even as James penetrated me, snaked his hand between our hot, sweating bodies to rub and stroke my swollen clitoris, a small voice of my conscience said what I was doing was wrong.

But it had been so long since I felt truly desired. Not admired like my husband had demonstrated to me, but truly desired. As if this man wanted nothing more in the world than me, and only me.

Just as I had lost count of the amount of times I came upon my former student's cock, I can't recall the number of positions and ways we fucked. Atop of him, feeling his eyes and hands roaming my body as I lowered myself upon him. Beneath him, pinned between his body and the bed as his cock pressed deeper and deeper within me. Behind me, his cock unleashing the full torrent of his hot, thick load.

Was this what I was missing in my monogamous life? This liberating, satisfying feeling of being desired in such a visceral and ethereal way? I considered this as we lay together upon that hotel bed, our limbs and bodies intertwined in the hot aftermath of the moment. More than anything, I did not want the night to end.

But the morning came, and we said our goodbyes with surprising ease. He would go back to his promising life, and I back to mine, teaching children and raising my family. There are times when I feel a sense of regret, but I'll never forget that magical night.

pregnant pause

JENNIFER D. MUNRO

He kissed me goodbye, his hand on my Buddha belly. I spanked him, a mere tap, his left cheek vivid to my hand through his thin suit pants. "Promises, promises," he said, like he always did, but without his usual mocking tone.

The screen door closed between us. He took ginger steps down the driveway. Lately I'd been the one with a peculiar gait, so I savored the switch. He cocked his fanny and reached back to adjust his inseam, I suspect for my viewing pleasure as well as to ease his discomfort.

He didn't take the motorcycle, despite the clear weather. The vibrating saddle would've been too much after what I'd given him. Maybe I should have made him ride the bike, a throbbing, over-the-speed-limit memory enhancer, every bump and pothole a deep-seated reminder of my affection.

Usually he swings himself into the four-by-four in one smooth movement. He inhabits his body with macho grace and ease, whether in jeans, a suit, or a skirt. But this morning he scooched himself backward up onto the seat with awkward caution. The sun's glare on the windscreen didn't hide his ecstatic flinch as his ass made contact with the seat. Again, maybe the performance was just for my benefit. I didn't care. I appreciated the show. After all, I hadn't gotten to see much of his face last night.

I confess. I am seven and a half months pregnant. And last night I butt-fucked my husband.

I know. I need to learn to watch my language. My mother-in-law would be appalled.

Doggie humping him in my gravid state wasn't easy. I struggled not to roll back on my butt like a wobbled Weeble, pulled out of him by the gravitational weight of my belly and the large mass of my ass, which had expanded as rapidly as my uterus. For leverage, I propped myself up against the bolster purchased for my prenatal yoga course. I wedged the firm pillow against the wall behind me and re-engineered my rear-flank assault. I liked this pose much better than the bladder-strengthening *asanas*.

My husband was very accommodating in his movement and positioning. He had waited out the protracted abstinence of my pregnancy without complaint. I hadn't felt an erotic charge since I started throwing up the day after conception. I couldn't even *see* my bush anymore, much less be in tune with it. No, my resolve to do this was to please him. More of a joke than sex. I needed to connect. To close the distance between us—when we hugged, we had to lean in over my protruding belly to kiss. He'd deprived himself of masturbation for months, wanting the sympathy pain to bond us. Cut off from our shared sexuality, he was a phantom limb—with a raging itch. Now that I'd scratched his suppressed arousal, inflaming his mind's erotic rash, he wasn't about to give up over minor logistics. I couldn't see his face, but I knew he was in ecstasy.

The power of the fucking unleashed an anger that surprised me. His cock, his sperm, had transformed me, incapacitated me.

Made me puke and waddle and swell. Made me a public artifact, people thinking they had the right to touch my ballooning belly as if it weren't my body, as if it weren't personal. Rammed me into a gender-specific role we'd spent our decade of marriage refuting, trading roles and holes once we crossed the bedroom threshold. Trapped me in the inexorable biology of my body despite my having thwarted sexual expectation since saying, "I do." Made me helpless and vulnerable, needing seats on buses, assistance down stairs, and a frigging potty break every three seconds. He had to drive me everywhere: once we pushed the seat back far enough to accommodate my girth behind the steering wheel, my feet wouldn't touch the pedals.

This thrust of my hard shaft in his tender ass—near-virginal after so much time—burst through months of built-up resentment like a pricked balloon. I was rough. Not nice. I wielded my cock with no care, taking my hostility out on him.

He'd complained about my sissy dominance in the past. He said I twittered when I spanked, I didn't pinch or bite hard enough, my knots were too loose. Blah blah fucking blah. Well, he didn't bellyache last night. I was the boss, a queen bee with a personal grudge and a wicked stinger. There was no giddiness, no fear of hurting if I went too deep, too hard, too fast. I wanted him to pay for my suffering. One peep and he would have been grateful for too tame, too timid, too easy. Fuck him and his teasing "Wimp" all those years.

He howled. I can't think what else to call the noise he made. I don't think he knew what planet he was on, his mind concentrated on the small hole I violated and abused, and yet far away, in a distant galaxy conjured by pain and pleasure. He protested a couple of times, but I told him without giggles to shut up and take it. He did. He needed to come. He was desperate for it, in fact. Wild for my hand.

I had trussed up his balls and cock in the O-ring he'd purchased at the hardware store. I'd had to get the metal band on quick, he'd gotten hard so fast at the sight of me when he walked in the front door. I'd strapped on a major household appliance we'd never used before—a dildo we'd christened "Goliath" for good reason. He knew what the monster strap-on meant. I'd never had the guts to penetrate the man I love with something so ugly and stupendous. Getting the damn thing on with no waistline was a feat of genius; I could see only the swirled-purple tip over the Vesuvius of my abdomen. At the sight of the Corinthian column sprouting from below my belly, rooted in the curlicues of my pubic hair, his eyes went wide. But not as wide as his ass had to be to take it.

I'd buckled his collar on, too, the one that's always been a little too tight. I didn't attach a leash; I grabbed his hair. Usually I followed his cues even when he was mine to use and abuse. But not last night.

"No," I told him, just like I say it to the dog, firmly, and only once, as the obedience school trainer instructed, "So your pet knows you mean it the first time." He reached for his cock. My husband, not the dog, that is, but what's the difference?

"No!" I said.

He reached to tug at the collar. "No!"

He reached back for me. "No!"

He even said "please." He'd never said that before, not while on all fours. I always gave him what he wanted before he had to ask. But, *click*, I got it this time. He wanted it, yes, he needed it, oh, yeah, but he wanted to beg even more. My pliancy had always denied him part of our passion play. I decided to make him beg until he was hoarse. To provoke his pleas until his asshole was sore, so that he remembered this union of bodies for days. Every time he sits, bends, walks, pees, or shits, the searing memory of the sex that created his discomfort will come back to him with a jolt. As it does to me.

I'm aware that we looked ridiculous. I'm also aware that if the neighbors ever caught sight of us, Child Protective Services would be hauled in. The authorities would make advance plans to confiscate the baby (we've chosen not to know the gender; there'll be time enough for those expectations later). But they would have banished us from neighborhood Block Watch potlucks years ago if they had peered through our bedroom blinds. They wouldn't understand that this fucking helps ensure that we will still be together, husband and wife, man and husband, woman and wife, creatively intertwined until orgasm do we part, for this child's high school graduation.

This is a wanted pregnancy, long-awaited. Why else would I keep a stick I've peed on as a souvenir of one of the happiest days of my life? So I didn't expect to uncork anger—anger I'd hidden even from myself—as I both unplugged and corked *his* dam of frustration. A dune of resentment had built up inside me, keeping us apart as much as the sickness, the fragility, the fear, the doctor's cautions. The fucking eroded the barriers, brought me back to center point like a compass. Just as my physical body was off center, off balance, so was my mind, my perception of myself. I craved a good dose of yang for my yin. I needed his wide-open, vulnerable body splayed beneath me, just as I have been wide open and vulnerable ever since the missionary-position sex, lying with my ass hiked up on a pillow to aid the heroic journey of the sperm, which created this life inside me. I needed him trembling under my thrusts, my catharsis for having surrendered my body to an alien being.

A thrill of power coursed through my loins, power stripped from me when his invasive sperm rammed my passive egg. A vengeful, domineering, raw power, capable of sending him to the guillotine, the lions, the cross…stripped naked, tortured into humiliating public hardness, and on the verge of perpetually denied orgasm. The occasional Braxton Hicks contraction I'd experienced lately, my body preparing for labor, was nothing compared to the rocket-takeoff orgasm that hit me. He whimpered when I blasted off from his launch pad, jealous that I allowed myself the searing, keening pleasure I denied him.

Did I let him come? Heavens, no. I want to whack his piñata as long as possible before the candy tumbles out. I still haven't let him. I'll make him wait until I'm good and ready and in the mood…after he has enslaved himself enough to understand what it's like to invite a tadpole to morph inside you. Whether it's embryo- or woman-with-a-dick-sized, the control is complete.

Besides. He likes it.

I know from the wink, the sheepish grin he flashed me as he backed out of the driveway this morning. His wedding ring glinted in the sun as he waved goodbye. I waved back with placid, matronly affection, my expectant silhouette unmistakable through the screen door. It's been so long since I have seen him so glowing, so radiant… but they say that's what pregnancy will do for you.

DELILAH NIGHT

The woman in the mirror was a stranger to me. When was the last time I'd changed my shirt? I surreptitiously took a whiff, and winced. There was a mystery stain on the hip of my shorts. The bags under my eyes might best be described as luggage. I had stopped wearing earrings after Liz had yanked one so hard I'd seen stars from the pain. My hair was dull and even my naturally curly hair looked tired—ringlets blurred into a fuzzy poof.

I dialed my best friend. "Jen, why didn't you tell me I look like hell?"

"You look like the mom of two kids under the age of three. Which you are. You don't need me critiquing your fashion choices. If you're so upset, buy yourself a new dress, ask your sitter to watch the kids a bit longer and get a pedicure or a massage or something. Don't beat yourself up. Gotta go—*Nathaniel Addison Massi*, put that down *now*!" The line went dead.

The woman in the mirror wouldn't greet her man on his birthday by lounging nude on a plastic tarp with several open containers of frosting and sprinkles nearby. She looked like the kind of woman who would yell at her kids for opening a can of frosting behind her back and spilling sprinkles on the floor.

It was time to reclaim myself.

dam had been weaned for over a month. I glanced around the empty bathroom, reached back, and undid the monstrous clasps of my nursing bra. The liberation of my breasts from their ugly polyester prison sent a frisson of happiness through my body.

As I left the bathroom, I thrust the nursing bra into the trash.

Justin and I met in college. He was a focused business major determined to make it on Wall Street. I was a dreamy history major more interested in learning about the history of women and sex than in any practical application of that knowledge post-graduation.

At first glance, we looked totally wrong for each other. He was tall and fit. I was short and all curves. His hair was ruthlessly groomed, while mine corkscrewed in every direction. Even as an undergraduate, Justin was rarely seen without a tie. I owned nothing that needed dry cleaning, and I had long since eschewed bras as too restrictive.

There was something magnetic that kept pulling us together, though. A shared fondness for Mel Brooks movies bordering on the obsessive, taking long drives to nowhere in particular while we talked non-stop, and the way we scraped money together all semester to travel all summer somehow braided our souls. Or at least that's what it felt like at twenty-three.

Justin's buttoned up exterior was a mask worn by a man whose family motto was "what will the neighbors/members of our synagogue think?" He was never to get too dirty or come home too late. It was unacceptable to have a less than stellar report card. If he did an extracurricular activity, he'd better become the president/star/captain.

Justin wasn't the sort of person who'd color outside the lines, so my slapdash approach to life was alien to him.

"Do you want to lick this off?" I giggled on our third date, gesturing to the melting bit of ice cream that had fallen into my cleavage. Little did I know the monster I was about to unleash. That one act—messy, uninhibited, and full of laughter— invited him through a door he never wanted to close again.

His new-found sexual adventurousness discovered a matching spirit in my own. The way he'd raise one eyebrow and grin at me was responsible for all manner of naughty diversions: sex in a bathroom at his little sister's bat mitzvah, both of us making out with a statuesque brunette, and my impromptu performance during an amateur night at a strip club in Denver, to name a few.

When we moved to New York after graduation, he worked crazy hours. But no matter how late he worked the first thing he'd do after getting home was to crawl into bed with me. He'd wake me with his mouth, his fingers, his cock.

Marriage hadn't changed a thing for us, at least not at first.

"Want to go to Power Exchange? The sex club? We can just watch," he murmured as he nuzzled my neck on our second anniversary. "Fifteen minutes. If you're not comfortable, we leave. It's our vacation, so let's do something crazy."

I clutched his hand as we entered the building. Justin encouraged me to direct our exploration. Following moans of pleasure, I led us down into the dungeon. My breasts and legs were complimented by more than one of the other patrons.

Watching a lusty blonde with three men made me wet. Justin nuzzled my neck. Moments later I turned and pushed him against the wall, kissing him frantically. Justin's hand darted into my panties, teasing my clit.

"I want to do something," he murmured as I widened my stance, giving him better access to my pussy.

"What?" I was willing to try almost anything if he'd keep doing that.

"Let me spank you."

My eyes, which had been shut to better focus on the stirring orgasm, flew open. "What?"

His hand moved to squeeze my ass. "There's plenty of people here who'd love to spank that ass of yours, but only I can. Let me make them jealous."

"Jealous?" I liked the way the word tasted in my mouth.

"Jealous."

I nodded my consent. Justin led me to a red plush couch and sat down in the middle. He patted the spot next to him. I knelt, then allowed him to bend me over his knees. One of his hands braced my body. The other caressed my legs before lifting my skirt to expose my green lacy panties.

I braced, waiting for the strike. I was surprised when his fingers slid beneath the lace and danced over my clit. Relaxing into the strokes of his fingers, I let Justin toy with me. I completely forgot the public aspect of our play until I heard a strange voice ask if Justin would lower my panties to show off my cunt. I felt the cool air of the room caress my skin as Justin complied.

"Beautiful girl you have there," the voice said. "Can I?"

I tensed up, worried for a moment what might happen next.

"Sorry, she's mine," Justin replied.

I relaxed again. Justin wouldn't let anything happen to me that I didn't consent to.

"Do you like knowing you made a stranger hard at the sight of you?"

I became even wetter, and he chuckled. His hand withdrew from my panties. I wondered what he would do next when his palm landed with a sharp smack on my ass.

"Naughty girl, aren't you?" This was our code, his way of asking if I wanted to continue.

"Yes," I whispered.

"Louder," his voice grew sharper as his hand came down again.

"Yes, I'm your naughty girl. I like it," I moaned when a staccato rain of slaps landed.

I was rewarded with long teasing strokes on my clit, and fingers thrusting into my cunt. Alternating waves of pain and pleasure. My behind burned with the same hot fire that was making my clit pulse.

SLAP!

"Are you a slut?"

SLAP! SLAP! SLAP!

"*Yes!* Please, Justin…" I begged, my eyes wet from a mixture of desire and pain.

"What?"

"Let me fuck you," I whimpered.

His hands moved and I was free. Shakily, I stood and reached toward the bowl of condoms sitting on a table nearby. A strange hand passed me one. I thanked them absently as, transfixed, I watched Justin open his jeans and free his cock.

I straddled and sheathed him, uncaring if the entire population of California was watching. Hungrily, I rode him. The orgasm hit me with the force of a category five hurricane, sending my hips into a frenzy. Justin groaned as he came moments later.

We both were a bit disoriented at the spattering of applause from the small audience we attracted.

"Thank you," he murmured.

In never forcing or demanding that I try anything, Justin made it safe to try everything.

Then things changed.

Maybe it was the move to Asia three years ago. It's possible that Singapore, with its sexual conservatism was exactly the wrong place for Justin. He slipped back into that quiet and socially correct armor he'd discarded back in college. Armor that created distance between us.

Perhaps it was having Liz not long after we arrived, and then Adam eleven months later. *Breastfeeding is effective birth control, my ass.*

Isolation from our friends and family, ten thousand miles and twelve time zones away didn't help.

These days, when Justin walked through the door, there were no enthusiastic kisses or gropes for me. He'd play with our kids as I tried to give an abbreviated recap of the day and reheated his dinner. We'd put the little ones to bed and then he'd want to zone out in front of the TV with me. Most nights I didn't even rate a goodnight kiss.

On weekends, he'd either "pop into work for a few hours" (*translation: the whole day*) or we'd take the kids out to Gardens by the Bay, the Zoo, the beach, or any number of indoor play spaces. Regardless of the activity, the focus was on our family, not *us*. When our babysitter came two Saturdays a month, he treated it as permission to go out with some work buddies and encouraged me to see my friends.

In bed, after he thought I'd fallen asleep, I could feel the mattress vibrate as he jerked off to porn on his iPhone. When we did have sex, it was the kind of paint-by-numbers rut that I'd always sworn we would *never* let ourselves fall into.

Today, though, I was a woman on a mission. I started on the top floor of Ion Orchard Mall and systematically began to shop. I needed pretty clothes, earrings, makeup, and more. I studiously ignored shorts and tank tops. I pretended flip flops didn't exist. Several hundred dollars later and with far too many bags to take on the subway, I stood in the taxi queue.

Once home, I made my selections from the purchases and packed a bag. I kissed my napping toddlers, and thanked my sitter profusely for her willingness to keep an eye on them overnight.

The room I checked into at Marina Bay Sands was the kind of hotel suite we couldn't afford in college. It was everything we'd pictured when talking about how one day *we'll really make it and can blow money on nice rooms and sexy trips.* The kind of room inside which we'd planned to fuck all day. I couldn't remember the last time we'd had sex twice in one day, much less spent a whole day screwing our brains out.

I spent two hours waxing, tweezing, and exfoliating my mom bod into a close approximation of my former self. My new panties and dress reminded me of the femininity I'd forgotten.

I sat by the window and watched the sunset casting a golden hue over the bay, the Merlion, and the city, contemplating my options.

Divorce? I still love him. Crappy sex? Great father. When had we last laughed together? He'd never cheat on me.

Round and round went my thoughts like the Singapore Flyer.

I called Justin. Shocked that I wanted him to meet me in a hotel room, he left work without protest or a request for another hour or three to finish whatever scraps of work he had left.

When I heard the knock on the door, I still wasn't sure what I wanted to ask for.

"Cara, I don't understand…" He took two steps forward. His tongue wet his lips as he reached out to trace the neckline of the sundress. "What's this? I've never seen this before…"

I stepped back. "Justin, we need to talk."

His posture went rigid. If anything, his tie looked tighter. His face relaxed into a neutral expression. I could have been talking to our accountant for all the personal connection he projected, with one exception. His eyes were practically burning a hole in my dress.

"I need more," I blurted out. "I used to lust for you. I'd look at your hands and remember them sliding under my skirt at that movie we saw on our fourth date. I'd see your dimples and remember all the stuff you talked me into…remember Cabo? Now it's like you're a stranger. But I feel like a stranger, too. We're two strangers."

I desperately needed him to understand.

As I talked, Super Corporate Guy fell away. Justin leaned against the wall, hands in his pockets, lips quirking in small smiles at the memories. "Strangers?" He rolled the word around in his mouth, testing its flavor.

I nodded.

"If you were my wife, I'd tell you that I'll work harder on us. That I love you. But you're a stranger." He prowled in a circle around me, his voice growing deeper.

"That's right. I'm a stranger. And you're here for one reason.". My clit swelled and the tops of my thighs grew slick.

"You're the kind of woman who'd summon a stranger to a hotel room for that?" he asked. "For this?" His hand slid over my breast, pinching my nipple for emphasis.

That touch sent a long missing ripple through my body. I hesitated, hoping he'd remember what I love. The pinch grew harder until I gasped, then changed to a rhythmic back and forth against the erect nub hungry for that exact touch. My eyes closed with pleasure. He leaned forward and nibbled on my neck, his finger still at work on my breast, his other hand sliding down to cup my ass.

"Yes…" I hissed with pleasure.

Suddenly he was kissing me, and he wasn't a stranger anymore. He was the man I've loved for more than a decade, and he was playing stranger in the hotel room with me. We were playing. We were connecting. The sexual heat that had been banked for who knew how long came roaring back to life.

I wrapped my hand in his tie, creating a leash, and pulled him to his knees. "I'm also the kind of woman who wants an orgasm. *Now*," I growled the last word.

He lowered my panties. Justin nudged my legs apart, and I pulled him close, draping a leg over one of his shoulders. His fingers parted my lips. His tongue teased my slit, coming close to, but not touching the swelling bud. I wrapped the tie around my hand again to pull him close, and Justin chuckled. Finally, his tongue flicked out in a motion that caused my knees to buckle, and my hand released the tie.

Justin lowered me to the floor. Pushing the skirt of the sundress to my waist, he returned to my pussy. I could feel the world shrinking to encompass only my cunt and his tongue.

"Pleasepleasepleaseplease," I panted as I arched up against his mouth.

"You're being naughty." He sat up, and I watched as his hand went to his tie. He slowly and deliberately untied it. "If you can't let me take care of you like a good little slut, I'm going to have to restrain you."

I shivered with delight. "Do whatever you think you have to."

He arched an eyebrow, and his dimples winked at me. I couldn't recall the last time I'd seen that particular smile. Soft silk whispered promises as he tied a knot Houdini would be hard pressed to escape from. My hands were raised over my head and Justin secured the other end of the tie to one of the desk legs.

Satisfied that I was adequately restrained, Justin returned to my wet quim. Lying between my thighs, he took a moment to look at me.

"It's been so long since you let me," he began, almost wistfully, slipping out of character.

"I've never let you do this," I reminded him even as I wondered at his word choice. When was the last time he'd been interested? That he'd asked to go down on me? That he hadn't bothered asking for permission and woke me up with oral?

"Right. But you're going to let me tonight, aren't you?"

"Yes!"

His tongue followed the same familiar pattern of teasing and reward that I lusted for. My pelvis undulated with his lips and tongue in a dance so well remembered that even as the steps changed, the partnership was seamless and beautiful.

I closed my eyes and let the pleasure wash through me, building from small lapping waves to roaring tsunamis, threatening to break down any and every barrier I'd erected or I'd allowed Justin to build. When I came, the game was over, because it was Justin's name that I screamed.

He gave me a few moments to lie there, senseless, feeling aftershocks ripple through my body. I didn't need to open my eyes to know he was smiling.

"This is new?" he asked, running his fingers contemplatively over the buttons that flowed from neckline to hem of the sundress.

"Yes," I breathed, barely able to open my eyes.

"I hope you didn't pay much for it," he said.

Justin gathered a handful of the dress in each fist and tried to dramatically rip my dress open like men did all the time in romance novels and porn. The fabric didn't give.

"What's this made of? Titanium?"

The failure of that move, rather than darkening the moment, inspired gales of laughter. Laughter had always been one of the ways we connected. More layers of distance peeled away. I began to see not just my lover but my best friend reappearing before my eyes.

"Defeated by a dress," he said finally, still gasping with laughter. He lowered himself to lie next to me.

His hand caressed the length of my still bound arms. He didn't offer to untie me and I didn't ask him to.

"You might try unbuttoning it," I suggested saucily.

"Indeed," he murmured, clever fingers already at work. "And what have we here? No bra? *How scandalous*," the last said with a teasing grin. *Scandalous* was his mother's word of choice to describe my bra-less state.

"You know, you could actually be doing something productive with that smart mouth of yours."

"Like apologizing?" His hand slipped in and fondled my breast, rubbing his thumb over my nipple. He still remembered how sensitive they were post-orgasm.

"I have a feeling that might be a mutual activity. I haven't really been there for you all that much lately, either."

He kissed me gently at first, his lips barely brushing mine. Changing the angle, he deepened the kiss, tongue flicking out to caress my lips, persuading them to give him entry. His hand caressed my cheek, and slid into my hair as he kissed me with every ounce of passion I thought he lost for me. I returned it with the same urgency and ardent desire.

"There you are," I whispered.

"Here I am," he agreed. "I love you, Cara."

"I love you too, Justin. Make love with me."

He smiled and whispered in my ear, "I hope you brought condoms. I love those two, but I'm not up for number three. I'm scared of going commando."

"Look in the drawer."

The size of the box made him laugh again. "I hope you weren't planning to use all of these tonight. You'd wring me dry, woman."

"They're a promise." I met his eyes.

"To…"

"To make an effort not to lose this again."

"I like that promise." He returned to the floor. "Now prepare to be ravished."

Justin nuzzled my neck as his hands made short work of the last few buttons on my dress. He took his time, exploring every inch of skin, making me sigh and moan. My frustration mounted. With the exception of his tie, he was still fully dressed.

The starched cotton of his shirt was at odds with the softness of his hands. He used the contrast to his advantage, intent on the task at hand. I could feel his cock straining towards freedom, but could do nothing besides beg for him to do me, and arch my hips.

"It's been too long since I've made you come," Justin murmured. "You're just going to have to tolerate several more orgasms."

"Oh, the horror," I joked.

His fingers slipped between my thighs, dipping into my hot core, testing and teasing until he found my g-spot. Massaging it, he reminded me of sexy times from our past.

"Do you remember when we played mini-golf for your panties? The hand-job you gave me as you were driving that rented sports car down Highway 1? The Petite Theatre in Paris? The time you flashed the window girl in Amsterdam?"

The sexy memories flashed through my mind in time with his fingers. The familiar pressure built again. When the orgasm hit me, I heard an audible crash. I'd moved the heavy wood desk enough for the phone to fall off.

The laughter bubbled up in me. When our eyes met, I couldn't keep it stifled any longer. He buried his face in my shoulder and laughed with me. We each would calm down a little, but the second our eyes met, we'd start laughing again.

Shaking his head, Justin got up to hang up the receiver and place the phone back on the desk. It rang. He frowned and picked it up.

"Hello? No, everything's fine." The wicked smile returned, "Just making love to my gorgeous wife. Goodnight."

If it hadn't already felt like I was floating a few inches above my body, I would have sworn I'd had an out of body experience. My proper workaholic husband had bragged to a stranger that he was doing me?

"You've been as lost as I've been," I realized out loud.

He untied my hands. We moved to the bed.

"Yes. I saw how hard it was with the baby. Then when stuff looked like it was settling down with Liz, you got pregnant again. I figured the best thing I could do was be a good dad and help out. Not be another strain on you. I know you don't get enough sleep, or much time with your friends without the kids. I figured sex was the last thing you'd want to use energy on, all things considered."

"I thought you didn't want me anymore because I looked like a mess and…" my voice trailed off.

"Baby, there isn't a day when I don't want you. I want you as much as I ever have. More."

"I want you, too," I said, slowly unbuttoning his shirt, kissing each inch of skin as it became exposed.

"Cara," he whispered, then moaned as my tongue flicked across a dark nipple.

I opened the buttons at his wrists and pushed the shirt from his shoulders. Encouraging him to lie down, I straddled his hips, feeling his erection beneath his dress slacks. I played with his chest hair, stroking it, tugging it, kissing down the love trail it made from his chest to his waistband. I licked his earlobes, his neck, and his nipples.

I took one of his hands and, meeting his eyes, suckled his middle finger, taking its full length into my mouth. Beneath me, his hardness jumped in echoing need. I rolled my hips to tease him as I sucked the finger.

"Cara," he moaned, dragging out the second syllable like a prayer.

I moved to kneel beside him and unbuckled his belt. His hands fisted in the duvet as I took my time with the waistband and inched down his zipper. Justin's cock threatened to break free of his boxers.

I smiled like a cat with a full bowl of cream as I stroked him through his boxers.

"Cara, I'm not Superman."

As I slid down pants and boxers, his dick sprung free to demand its fair share of attention. I bent to lick the head, swirling my tongue around it. Justin swore with pleasure as he fought the urge to come. I fondled his balls as I licked my way up and down his shaft. A finger slipped back to tease and press on his taint, as I took him into my mouth.

An expert multi-tasker, I opened the box of condoms and extracted one. I replaced my mouth with the condom before straddling Justin. Our eyes locked as I lowered myself onto him. My cunt stretched to accommodate him, and my eyes closed with pleasure.

My hips rocked with increasing urgency. As if it had only been moments instead of months, my body knew exactly the right rhythm, the right pace to let the orgasm build and then explode in my body. I heard Justin gasp my name as he came.

I let my body still, and we were motionless for a few moments, letting pleasant aftershocks dash through our bodies. I gingerly lifted myself off him, careful to keep the condom in place. He was equally cautious in removing it, both of us treating the sperm like potentially dangerous prisoners. There would be no number three today.

Lying in the king-sized bed, we talked and laughed long into the night. In the morning, Justin called out sick, and we spent it in bed renewing our commitment to each other. When it was time to check out, we headed home to our children, eager to find the balance between his work, our own interests, our love, our lust, and our family.

a desperate state

CECILIA DUVALLE

Connie pressed her forearm against her mouth, muffling her moan as she came. Her free hand pulled at Jake's hair to lift his head, telling him to ease up. He looked across her sweaty stomach and breasts and placed his dripping chin on her mons, a huge grin plastered across his face. She had no doubt that he loved her pussy.

She guided him up over her body, reaching between his legs. "Your turn."

It was a Thursday, aka "missionary night." It was part of an unspoken pattern they had developed over the last few years. Connie lifted her hips to greet him as he moved in and out of her with practiced ease. They both froze as the headboard hit the wall with the motion. They shifted lower on the bed and slowed their pace. The last thing they wanted was to announce their activities to the whole house. He came after another dozen noiseless thrusts. She caressed his head as he hovered over her, staying inside her to prolong the moment.

Connie kissed him before he rolled off her, murmuring an *I love you* as he pulled her into position against his side. She tucked her head against his shoulder, exhausted and ready to sleep. Jake's breathing shifted into slow hushed snores, and she wished, once again, she could get to sleep as quickly as he could. What was it? Thirty seconds from fucking to sleeping?

Just as she was finally fading into sleep, a knock on their door jolted her awake.

"Mom? Dad? There's something wrong with the printer." A rattle of the door confirmed it was locked. "Guys? You awake?"

Jake continued snoring. The man could sleep through a freight train. Connie kissed him on the cheek and sat up, grieving the loss of the moment.

"Coming, Kara, just give me a minute," she said. Connie slipped out of bed and rushed into the bathroom to wipe up and toss on a robe. Their teenager's sleeping pattern, or lack thereof, was frustrating in more ways than one.

Kara was leaning against the doorjamb waiting when Connie opened it. She ran fingers through her hair and shot Kara a slightly perturbed look.

"Wasn't interrupting something gross, was I?" Kara asked, the revulsion found in virgin teendom wrinkling across her brow. She turned and led the way down the hall.

"Were you standing at the door listening?' Connie asked. 'It's not like you don't have an iPod you know."

"Oh, stop. I'm out here working my ass off on homework, and you and Dad are fooling around. It's not like we need any more kids in this family, either." Kara was not fond of her weekly chore of babysitting her two younger siblings and lodged daily complaints about their general character and behavior.

It didn't take long for Connie to figure out what was wrong with the printer and show Kara how to fix the problem in the future. There were a lot of school reports yet to come from this young lady. She sighed when she looked at the clock. How had she become someone who looked at half-past midnight as being uber-late? Long-gone were the days when she ended a night out eating pancakes while watching the sun rise.

"Print and go to bed. That's an order."

"I just have a couple of calc problems to do. Then I'll go to bed. Half an hour at the most, I promise."

"Whatever. Just set your alarm so you aren't late for school tomorrow."

Connie checked in on the two younger kids on her way back to bed. Even they were staying up until eight or nine at night. Her bedtime had grown later and later just to have any free time to read, watch television, or just be with Jake. Sex had become a hushed and predictable routine.

It hadn't always been missionary on Thursdays and doggie-style on Saturdays. When they were first married, Connie would meet Jake at the door, pull him into their apartment and fuck him before dinner—standing in the hallway, leaning against the kitchen counter, bending over the back of the sofa. They'd eat, find a new position on a different piece of furniture or in another corner of their apartment, then maybe go to their bedroom for more.

When they moved into the new house ten years ago, Kara was still sleeping a blessed twelve hours a night. The house was their sexual playground for a while. Then the other children came along, and the minutiae of daily life ate away their free time. Sex became something that happened in their bedroom with the door locked, her pillow or arm shoved against her mouth.

Connie paused as she passed the living room, and the memories of their childless freedom welled up in her. Her eyes locked on the overstuffed chair. She craved the sex they used to have on it, her knees sinking onto either side of the cushion, his cock buried deep inside her and hitting her cervix in a painfully pleasurable way. Just looking at the sofa had her ready for another round with Jake. She decided then and there that she would, somehow, manage to capture that freedom again. Time alone with Jake. *At home.*

Getting an evening alone with Jake required a lot of wrangling, but it would be worth the effort. Once she started thinking about all that free-form-all-over-the-house-sex, she burned for immediate satisfaction. She returned to her bedroom, shutting the door a little louder than necessary. Jake's snoring shifted to a louder gear as he rolled over, and she knew he wasn't going to wake up easily. She climbed into bed and poked at him, but his gurgled snores merely paused for a second. When was the last time they'd had sex twice in one night?

She pulled out her vibrator and placed the tip against her clit. She just needed one more quick orgasm so she could get to sleep. She dialed it up until the vibe was at maximum. She pictured Jake on his back in the warmth of the window seat, full sunshine on his chest making his skin glow, her mouth engulfing his cock. The strength of the vibe and the simple image had her coming in less than a minute. She tossed the vibe back into the drawer and pulled the covers up over her shoulders. As she fell asleep, Connie started making a mental list of all the favors various family and friends owed her that could be cashed in. She was determined to get some housebound rampant sex with her husband.

The next morning, she met Mary at the gym. As they bounced side by side on their elliptical trainers, Connie brought up her plan.

"Get out of town," Mary said. "Why go to all the effort of getting the kids out of your hair only to stay at home?"

It was clear that Mary didn't *get it*. She and her husband, Noel, were committed to their no-kid lifestyle. They had never experienced rigidity enforced by domestication and progeny. They lived in a downtown condo, regularly picked up and flew to other parts of the world, and had no idea how regular people really lived. If it weren't for the fact that Connie and Mary had grown up together they'd have nothing in common.

"No way! If we go out of town, we'll be in a hotel. Hotels just have a bed, a chair or two, and maybe a table. At home, we have sofas, chairs, stairs, this amazing ottoman in the office, the piano, the kitchen table, the counter. Access to the freezer and a bunch of toys that would fill a suitcase. Things that would make the TSA blush or get us arrested."

"Oh…" she said, drawing the sound out as comprehension dawned. "I think I'm going to have a hard time choosing where to sit next time I come over there."

Connie rolled her eyes and took a long swig from her water bottle. Connie punched the level up a couple of notches. Mary startled her by grabbing her wrist and stopping dead-still. Connie dropped her own gait and looked at her friend with concern.

"Wait…did you say freezer?"

The look on Mary's face was priceless. Connie laughed before she looked around to make sure there weren't others listening in before continuing. People at her gym were usually plugged into their mp3 players or the screens on their machines, but she didn't like the idea of people overhearing what she was about to say. If Mary looked scandalized, she guessed the other old biddies that habituated the place would lose it entirely.

"You remember those rocket shaped popsicle forms I bought last year? I haven't even been able to use them yet." Connie paused, raising an eyebrow with intent. "At least not for the reason I really got them for."

"What? Wait, you put popsicles in your…" Mary dropped her gaze to her own crotch, her lips curling up and her eyes widening. She grabbed for the treadmill to steady herself.

"I use plain water. Fruit juice would cause no end of troubles, but it's a great shape and has a built-in handle."

"Damn, girl. That's just something I've never heard of." Mary shivered in mock exaggeration.

Connie waggled her eyebrows. She had completely stopped all motion, and both women stood on their machines leaning into each other. Moving in even closer to Mary, she said, "Yeah, but then, when I'm all really, really cold, and Jake starts to fuck me? It's like this totally hot burning cock inside me, and for both of us it's, well…the temperature differential is *amazing*."

Mary's mouth opened and closed a couple of times as if she couldn't quite find the words. Shaking her head, she said, "No one is coming near my va-jay-jay with ice. Nuh-uh."

"Don't knock it until you try it…and it's almost impossible to explain to three kids why the rocket shaped popsicles are filled with plain water. Trust me, they will notice and they will ask. I sure can't tell them the truth. I've been wanting to use them for an entire year and haven't been able to sneak it around them."

～

It took more than a dozen phone calls, one promise of a reciprocating sleepover and six shots of espresso before Connie had a plan in place-- not just for one night, but an entire glorious weekend. Given the immensity of the task and planning involved, it wasn't going to happen right away. That was okay with Connie. The intervening days before the event itself would act as extended foreplay.

She teased Jake with all her dirty plans. Dropping her hand to his balls, she'd cup them as she reminded him of how he liked to feel her mouth on them while he stood outside in the backyard, bare-naked to the world. She stroked his cock into hard readiness as her whispered desires fell quietly across his chest. Mounting him, she rode him while promising him a hard, fast, scream-inducing fuck in the middle of the living room.

"I love it when you used to lose it and just yell at me to pound into you harder, to fill you up," he said. "Will you scream for me?"

She promised him more than just a scream. The plan she had set in place broke their weekly rhythm, but not their silence and circumspection.

"I keep thinking about the time we discovered what a perfect height the coffee table is," she said one night. She slipped out of bed and draped herself across the edge, wiggling her naked ass in offering. He laughed and climbed out of bed. Pushing her stomach flat against the mattress he slipped into her from behind. They looked at each other's reflection in the mirror across from them as their bodies melded into each other in silence, their joint memory fueling their quiet reconstruction of days gone by.

She counted the days and marked an elaborate red "x" on the calendar every night before going to bed. Finally, the first day of The Week arrived--just five more days of the daily grind before their forty-eight hours of indulgence. Tuesday came and went in a flurry of regularity.

By Wednesday, Connie was dripping in expectation all day long. Everywhere she turned became a possible scene for sex--the laundry room, the kitchen, the garage. The front porch. Maybe the neighbors wouldn't notice them on the swing out front if they kept the lights off and the noise down low. The entire jungle-gym took on new dimensions. Too bad they didn't have a teeter-totter. Thinking about what she could do with one of those made Connie disappear into her bedroom with her favorite dildo for a good half hour. Even preparing dinner had its sexual overtones. Cucumbers morphed into cocks, potatoes into butt plugs, and the clink of ice against glass sent shivers through her body.

But then, on Thursday morning, Morgan--their youngest--woke up with a fever. Connie panicked. She had to keep her home for the day and fever-free for twenty-four hours before sending her back to school. Her previous weeks of thinking about sex shifted into panic. After the planning, the teasing, and the daydreaming she had done for the weekend, Connie was determined not to cancel. She had to have some loud sex with Jake.

She became Mama Nightingale, catering to Morgan's every need. She made her homemade chicken soup, hand squeezed orange juice, and gave her just the right amount of medication to take the fever away. When she woke her up in the middle of the night to make sure the medicine was on top of things, Connie felt a little prick of guilt. Morgan woke Friday morning as her chipper usual self with no sign of fever or having had one. Relief flooded through Connie as she realized the day had arrived and all her kids seemed healthy.

When Connie sent the kids off to school with their bags for their weekend away from home, she jumped and clicked her heels. She filled all six Popsicle molds with water. The weather was supposed to get pretty warm.

She did enough shopping that they could hole up in their house for the entire weekend. Sure, they'd need a break from the sex, but that didn't mean they would have to get dressed or be presentable if they didn't feel like it.

She layered her clothing to tease Jake. Over thigh-high stockings, lace panties and lace bra, she put on sweatpants and a dumpy soccer-mom sweater. When she heard the garage door open, she jumped onto the sofa with a book, trying to look bored in spite of the fact that her clit felt like a cantaloupe ready to explode.

"Honey, I'm home," Jake said. He rounded the corner into the living room and stopped when he saw Connie.

It was hard to keep a neutral face when she looked up from the book. "Oh…Hi! You're home early." She said it as if she had no idea why he was home at four o'clock in the afternoon.

He looked around the room as if expecting something to fall off the wall and then back at her. He narrowed his eyes and smiled. "You're funny."

Holding out his hands, he grabbed hers and pulled her into his arms. He felt around underneath her oversized shirt. "Ha!"

She laughed as he pulled the dowdy shirt over her head and tossed it to the side. He knew her too well. And just well enough.

"Ohhhh…black lace." His voice was muffled between her breasts as he lowered his lips to the cleft between them. He tugged at her sweats to reveal the matching black panties and stockings.

She wasn't sure when the last time was she'd stood in her own living room in such little clothing, but it sure felt like the first. He caught the cloth of the panties with a finger, pressing it up into her.

"Wet." He was a man of few words.

"Drenched, more like. It's not going to take much to get me to come right now." Her voice was low and hoarse, filled with hunger and promise.

He pulled the cloth out and pushed it in again before rubbing the liquid soaked fabric against her clit. Connie leaned forward and grabbed at his shoulders. It was hard for her to stand while coming without support. All the pent up, built up need in her spilt over quickly with this first orgasm. She smothered her moans against the lapel of his suit jacket.

Jake laughed. "So much for screaming out loud."

"Habits are hard to break." She tugged at his tie and flung it away before attacking the buttons of his shirt and his belt buckle. She grabbed at his cock through the layers of his trousers and briefs. "I can't wait to get you inside me."

"Oh, hungry for a good fuck, are you?" he asked.

"Definitely."

There was a subtle shift in his smile, and his eyes twinkled with a mix of mischief and humor. "I think you need to prove you can make it worth *my* while."

Connie paused in her groping, intrigued by the new game.

"Oh." Her lips curved upward. "What, exactly, do I need to do to prove myself to you?"

"I want you to let loose. Scream. Cry. Groan. Beg." He paused as if the last bit had come out without him planning on it. "I want you to beg me to fuck you. Be at your wits end, screaming in agony."

"Screaming in agony," she echoed.

"Well, not in pain…out of need," he clarified. But, he didn't alter his demand.

"You're going to need to build that up again, since you just got me off."

"I think that can be arranged."

She unzipped his pants and pushed all the intervening layers away from his body until the fabric pooled at his ankles. His cock bobbed out in full readiness and she dropped to her knees in front of him. She rubbed it along her cheek, savoring the smoothness of his skin.

Darting a tongue out to circle the head of his cock, she looked up at him as though daring him to not shove it in her mouth and come himself. He knew her too well, how easily she could be distracted.

"Didn't you say something about Popsicles?" he asked.

She was up in a second.

"Oh, yes! Let's start with that, shall we?" She ran into the kitchen. She was back with a bowl and one of the water-pops she had made earlier.

He chuckled as he motioned for her toward the sofa. She slipped off her panties and left her stockings on before sitting back and spreading her legs for him. He put the bowl on the floor next to him. "I think it needs a couple of minutes to melt first."

Placing his thumbs on either side of her labia, he spread her wide open, knelt between her legs, and just looked at her. Connie felt utterly and completely exposed in the full daylight of their living room.

"Beautiful." He leaned forward, gently licked her exposed clit with a single long stroke of his tongue, then leaned back.

Connie tried to push her hips up toward him but his thumbs pressed into her and kept her firmly against the sofa. "God, Jake. More."

Jake chuckled, his eyes ablaze with a fire she hadn't seen in a long time. Leaning in, he slid his hands along her thighs to her knees. He dropped his lips to her thigh just above the stocking and kissed her, but not quite just kissing. He sucked in a little bit of skin and nibbled it between his teeth, biting her. The throbbing in her pussy stepped up a few beats.

This was new. Connie stopped breathing. He dropped her flesh, and she released her breath. He looked up at her to check her reaction. The bright mark on her skin thrummed in unison with her pussy. A love-bite. Sucking in her lower lip, she nodded for him to continue.

Jake worked his way up her thigh, taking little bites and nibbles between kisses along the way. He lifted his lips from her skin and blew a gentle puff of air at her clit to tease her before jumping over to her other thigh.

Connie groaned in appreciation with each successive bite.

Once he had made his way down to the other stocking, Jake sat back and looked at his work. Six marks along each thigh burned bright against her creamy skin. Their eyes met, and Connie new that this was a game changer. They'd always had a little kink in their life, but this was taking things up a notch.

"More."

"Louder. I couldn't hear that."

"Jake," she said, not quite yelling, "Don't you think the ice is ready?"

Jake picked up the rocket-shaped icicle and held it up for inspection. A slick layer of water beaded along the surface, making it look like a glass dildo shining with lube. He ran the edge of it along her labia and she shivered, half in anticipation and half from the cold.

"Do you want me to fuck you with the popsicle, Connie?" He pressed the tip against her clit and ran it along her outer lips.

She shivered and pushed her hips upward toward the ice, but he snatched it away from her and held it over her dripping hole, half promise, half threat. "Yes. Please."

"I can't hear you." He sang it, like a child holding a ball away from another kid. He inserted the tip of the popsicle into her.

She groaned. "More, please."

Jake slid the popsicle all the way in and yanked it out. The sudden movement startled her, and left her aching for more. He wrapped his lips around the popsicle, cleaning off her juices. "Mmmmmm. Yummy."

"Please, Jake." Her voice caught on his name. She could barely speak.

He acted as though he had forgotten what he was doing. "What was that?"

She cleared her throat and put some force behind her words. "Damn it, Jake. Fuck me with the popsicle!" Her words echoed against the high ceiling.

Jake slid the popsicle across her clit before shoving it inside her. Connie sucked in a great gulp of air at the sensation. He swirled the popsicle around, making sure the frigid ice touched every bit of her insides, leaving it in a little longer with each stroke. Numbing her a little more with each stroke. His other hand fingered her clit to bring her closer to another orgasm. Her hips bucked against him in response. She knew she could come with what he was doing, but she would hold back until his flesh replaced ice. The only thing in the world she wanted was his scorching cock burrowing deep inside her.

"Jake. Fuck. Me."

"I don't think you're ready yet." He held back, clearly teasing her with his fully engorged cock just inches from her wet, frozen cunt.

"Fuck me, please. Drop the ice and just fuck me!" She shouted the order to the rafters. An exhilarating freedom filled her as the words left her mouth.

"What was that, dear?" his words were soft—coaxing, teasing.

Connie breathed in deep. Years' worth of silence filled her lungs, and her yell burst out of her like a warrior in the heat of battle. "Damn it, Jake. Get your cock in my pussy now."

The immediate freezing cold of the ice disappeared with a clink against metal. The heat of his cock against her lips was like a searing iron entering her, burning her, scalding her even though it was just hot flesh.

"Yes. Oh. My. God. YES!"

Jake plunged into her, bucking against her as she thrust her hips up toward him. The look on his face mirrored hers.

She urged him on, her voice rising in volume until she was maxed out. His cock continued to burn inside her with each thrust. The synergy of sensations built and grew until they came at the same time. Jake collapsed on top of her, his cock still inside. She stroked his head as he snuggled against her chest.

"Well, that's a good start," she said.

"I have a feeling you're going to be very sore by Sunday evening."

"Are you talking about my throat or my pussy?"

"Both."

"Now that," she said, wrapping her legs around him, "sounds like a plan."

waiting for ilya

TERESA NOELLE ROBERTS

"I'm in the kitchen," Tom called as Stacy walked in the door. "The steaks just went on."

On her way to the kitchen, she tossed her purse and well-thumbed copy of *Parenting your Internationally Adopted Child* onto a chair in the living room.

Two glasses of red wine perched on the shiny new kitchen counter. Tom was leaning against the counter, shirtless under a dark green apron that brought out the green in his hazel eyes.

Stacy took a second to stare. Busy as they'd been, she hadn't taken enough time lately to appreciate how hot and sexy her husband was—although she supposed that wasn't a terribly motherly thought and she should definitely work at thinking like a mom. "You must have gotten home early tonight. What's the occasion?"

"Do I need an occasion to open a bottle of wine and make a nice dinner?" Tom brandished the corkscrew dramatically.

"I guess not." She hoped she didn't sound suspicious but she was certainly surprised. They'd been focusing all their energy on the adoption and on getting their home ready for Ilya, and putting all their money into the house and the multiple trips to Russia required by the adoption agency. So wine and steak *did* feel like an occasion.

"It's Friday night." Tom set the corkscrew on the counter. "I figure we're past due for a date night, especially since we won't have a lot of chances for date nights soon, because we'll have a son." He grinned as if he wasn't much older than five-year-old Ilya himself. "Just three more weeks until we bring Ilya home! Isn't that enough of an occasion—that and I love you madly?" He drew her into his arms and into a kiss.

As the kiss blossomed on Stacy's lips, she remembered how Friday nights—and Tuesdays and Thursdays, for that matter— used to be. They hadn't planned on buying a house yet, not until the adoption was complete and Ilya had settled into life with his new family. But this one had been such a deal, and had such a big, beautiful yard—perfect for a child to run around and get healthy after his rough start in life—that they jumped on it even though it needed "a little work."

They hadn't comprehended how much work, on top of all the time and emotional energy going into the adoption.

They needed this night. They really did.

But they were on a timetable. Parents couldn't afford to be selfish. "We were going to work on Ilya's room tonight," Stacy said in a small, but persistent voice. They hadn't expected the adoption to be finalized before September, but a few days ago they'd gotten the good news they could return to Moscow in less than a month to bring home the little boy they'd come to love over the course of their visits to Russia—a delightful, yet daunting surprise. "He deserves a room of his own. Though I suppose," she reflected, "he might be happier in our room for a while. He's slept in a dormitory with a bunch of other kids his whole life. Being alone at night on top of all the other changes might be too scary."

"All the more reason to enjoy tonight. Having a child will be a big change for us, especially if he starts out sleeping in our room. A wonderful change, but it's going to cut down on date nights, not to mention spontaneous kinky sex. Better enjoy those things while we can."

Anger surged through her, protective fury for the child who was theirs in everything but the paperwork. Was Tom already complaining about parenthood when Ilya wasn't even with them yet?

As quickly as the anger rose, it subsided. Stacy knew the anger was just a cover for her own fears. Tom had a good point. Even now, just working to get the house ready for their child, she'd been a bit stressed and more than a bit horny, feeling like she shouldn't take the time to fool around with her husband, but definitely missing it. But wouldn't taking a night off for themselves, when Ilya was arriving so soon and the house was still a disaster area, be perilously close to saying they weren't ready for Ilya? That they didn't deserve Ilya?

"We're going to be parents at last. It will make our relationship stronger. We shouldn't worry about how it's going to affect our sex life." Her voice dropped to a whisper as she added, "But I do. I feel like I'm already letting it affect our sex life because I'm so nervous about making everything perfect for him. And then I feel like a horrible selfish person for even thinking that." To her horror, her lips quivered as she fought back tears.

Immature. Selfish. Ilya had already been abandoned by one set of parents who weren't able to put his needs first. At least his birth-parents might have had the excuse of being too young or too poor to take care of a baby. Stacy had no such excuse. They were nearly forty, supposed grown-ups with good jobs, though she was taking a long leave of absence and wasn't sure she'd end up going back. "Maybe I'm not ready for this," she confessed. "Maybe I never will be." Maybe their inability to conceive had been the universe's way of telling her that she wasn't cut out to be a mom, wasn't strong enough to make the necessary sacrifices.

"I think it's finally hitting you that cool as it is the adoption paperwork got fast-tracked, we're getting our kid a few weeks from now instead of a few months, and we're not as prepared as we'd hoped we'd be. Trust me, I already had my own freak-out. Hence the nice bottle of wine and the steaks. I figured we needed them."

For about the thousandth time in the turbulent adoption process, Stacy reflected she'd picked a good man.

And a very sexy one, although that was probably not the best thing to think at the moment, not when she was so shaky, not when she wasn't sure if she wanted sex or a good cry or possibly both.

Tom hugged her close, gave her another kiss. She tried to feel only the tenderness in the kiss, the love, but she couldn't help it. The heat was there too, and it sizzled into her. Her nipples crinkled and stood at attention. Her pussy twitched in anticipation. She pressed her breasts against Tom's chest, circling them a little to enjoy the slight stimulation.

Part of her felt like she should insist they get some work done on Ilya's room before they gave themselves license to play.

But the room would be there in the morning. They'd have plenty of time to paint and get the bright jungle-animal border up over the next couple of days.

Stacy's good intentions, Stacy's fears, Stacy's notions about how a mother should behave, were dissolving under Tom's kiss.

One of his hands cupped the back of her head, a subtle control that let her relax into the moment, into Tom's touch, into Tom's body. The other hand pushed up her skirt. She was barelegged on this fine spring day, and her skirt was short. It wasn't long before Tom's hand was sliding inside the lacy hip band of her panties, sliding along the curve of her ass.

Stacy adjusted her stance, spreading her legs to encourage that questing hand. Soon it gripped hard, a possessive gesture that sent a guilty thrill through her.

She felt even guiltier when Tom gave her butt a light slap—not even a spank, more an exploratory tap to see how she'd respond—and she moaned and thrust her butt back in blatant invitation.

She was a mom. Tom was a dad. Okay, their child wasn't living in the house yet, but they were Ilya's parents, or would be soon, just as if she was massively pregnant and eagerly waiting for her due date. What kind of decent parents got into spanking games?

The kind of parents they would be, apparently. It shouldn't have surprised her, although on some level it did. They'd dabbled in kink, enjoying spanking and light bondage and occasional experiments with something more fierce. Why had she thought they'd suddenly become vanilla?

If the thrill, the very primal need, coursing through Stacy was any indication, they'd find a way to play sometimes, even if it was late at night and at the opposite side of the house from where Ilya was sleeping. They'd have to. She wondered how much of her recent tension was anxiety about the adoption and how much was horniness, the need for a good spanking and a hard fuck that they simply hadn't taken the time to indulge in lately.

"I've been thinking we have to be June and Ward squeaky-clean Cleaver to be good parents," she said seemingly out of nowhere, knowing that Tom would get it. "But Ilya will be better off if we're just us and happy."

"Duh," Tom said, not unkindly. "Though I suppose we'll have to keep the sex in the bedroom instead of wherever we get the urge."

Then he spanked her again, harder this time, and before she could stop herself—before she could even remember why she thought she should stop herself—Stacy cried out, "Oh, God, I need that."

Tom whispered, "Take your panties off and lean on the counter."

The brand-new counter, the one they'd just finished installing last month.

Not that long ago, they'd have "broken in" the new counter right away, celebrating the renovation by seeing how many ways they could incorporate it into sex. With all they had going on, playing had slipped from the list of priorities.

Stacy felt a flash of sorrow about that, followed by a much bigger flash of lustful glee that it was happening now. The damn guilt tried to work its way back into her consciousness, but she made herself ignore it. Their little boy wasn't even in the country yet, let alone wandering in the kitchen to wonder why Daddy was spanking Mommy. Definitely no reason to feel guilty.

Before her overdeveloped sense of responsibility made her change her mind, Stacy slithered out of her panties, gyrating more than necessary to give Tom a good show. She braced herself against the counter, stuck her ass out, wiggled it at Tom.

Tom gently, slowly, teasingly raised her skirt, making the simple gesture a ritual. The fabric slithered against Stacy's skin. She bit her lip to stifle a groan of need.

He ran his hand gently over her thrust-out ass. At that point, Stacy stopped trying to stifle her moans. The sound came out deep and throaty, shocking her with its raw, blatant desire. After feeling they shouldn't fool around, Stacy was now frantic for it, as if her efforts at self-control had only served to arouse her more. Her pussy throbbed, her thighs felt slick and damp, and Tom's feather-light touch was making her crazy. Forget that—the touch of the air was making her crazy. "Please," she begged. "Please," her voice hoarse with need.

Tom's hand came down hard on her ass. Pain and pleasure ricocheted through her body, jarring loose the guilt, the fear that she wouldn't be a good mother, that she'd be too wrapped up in Tom and neglect Ilya. She wasn't sure where the guilt and fear came from. At some point, now that she could see how absurd it was, she'd take the time to trace it back to its roots.

Right now, though, she was going to let the spanking carry her away. Right now, she was going to stop thinking and ride the delicious combination of pleasure and thuddy pain.

Each smack brought her closer to Tom, not the dad-to-be counterpart to her mom-to-be, but the lover she'd married and chosen to become a parent with, the whole package she adored, including the kinks. The spanking and other minor fetishes were part of who they were together, a part of a love for each other so strong they knew they had to share it with a child who needed them. And they'd find a way to keep expressing their love for each other—their way—even while they made a safe and welcoming home for a child who'd never had one.

A particularly hard blow jarred her spine—jarred her heart, too, letting loose the last remnants of grief that another woman had carried their child, that she'd never give birth to a baby conceived in the fire of her passion for Tom. She hadn't realized she still harbored those regrets, thinking she'd replaced them with joy the first time Ilya smiled at them and said, in his labored English, "I love you." But maybe it was natural for grief and bliss to coexist, like pain and pleasure.

Tom spanked her several more times in rapid succession, too quick and hard for her to process immediately. It snapped her out of introspection and into orbit. Her drenched pussy gripped at nothing. She rode the rhythm of sharp shock transmuting to ecstasy, rode the waves of joy and panic triggered by Ilya's impending arrival, rode her love for Tom to a place where she laughed and cried and came all at once.

Crying, laughing, coming, she reached out for Tom and found he'd already unzipped his jeans. He slammed into her, his body slapping against her tender butt. At the same time, though, he kissed her neck and shoulder softly, sweetly.

Her pussy fluttered and squeezed at him, and she pushed back to meet his urgent thrusts. "Don't hold back," she whispered.

He didn't. It was a wildfire fuck, fast and urgent, each of them egging the other on until it almost hurt but instead was beautiful. At the end, as Tom came inside her and she exploded again along with him, Stacy swore she smelled burning.

Then she realized she *did* smell burning. "The steaks!"

Tom was laughing and cursing as he yanked his jeans up and hopped out the back door, still zipping up.

When Tom came back inside, he was shaking his head and still laughing. "The steaks are charcoal."

"I bet June Cleaver would never burn dinner because she was too busy fucking."

"Technically *I* burned dinner," Tom corrected her. "And I'm sure if Ward Cleaver forgot the steaks on the grill, he'd take June out for a nice dinner to apologize. How does sushi sound?"

"Perfect." She winked. "It's light enough that it won't weigh us down later. Quickies are good, but I imagine we'll be having a lot of those as parents. After dinner, I want to take our time."

toy story

ANDREA LANI

Kendra's husband's head was between her legs and she was thinking about rubber ducks. Charlie hummed a little like a happy child as he explored her with fingers, teeth, and tongue. She gripped his head, pulling him in closer, her hips shifting to meet him. Grit from the sheets chafed against her bare skin. Nothing she said could convince the kids that her bed was not a jungle gym, pirate ship, or bear cave. What had they dragged in this time? Cookie crumbs? Road salt from last week's snowstorm?

When the twins were born, Kendra and Charlie's bedroom had become a makeshift nursery, with bassinet, crib, and changing table crammed in the corners and washcloths, diapers, and rattles piled on every surface. Even after the boys moved into their own room, Charlie and Kendra had never really reclaimed their space. A broken Playmobil airport sat on her bedside table and a firetruck on Charlie's, its ladder extended, a little plastic man hanging from the lamp. At least it was only dirt and not a Lego grinding into her backside, Kendra thought. She wished she had bought a set of satin sheets or a filmy red canopy at the store her friend Julia had dragged her into while Christmas shopping in Portland a few days earlier. Anything to bring a little romance to the bedroom and draw her attention away from the crayon drawings scrawled on the sloping wall above her head.

The murmur of voices and the metallic clink of Legos down the hall alerted Kendra that the boys were up. She and Charlie had maybe five minutes before two pairs of fists came pounding on the bedroom door. She tried to focus her attention on the movement of Charlie's fingers and tongue, the soft scrape of his beard against her skin, but just as the first tingles of excitement began to radiate down her limbs, Charlie clambered up her body, commando-style, eager for his share of pleasure. He had just slipped inside her when the voices in the other room grew louder, the first tremors in a brotherly fight. Charlie made a few half-hearted thrusts, but with the sound of something large crashing to the floor and the wailing cry of at least one of the boys, he rolled off Kendra, yanked on a pair of sweats, and leaned down to kiss her.

"I'll take the boys down to make pancakes," he said. "You rest a while."

Kendra listened to the crying and recriminations, fighting her instinct to go in and fix things. After a moment, the sobs hushed and she heard three sets of footsteps thunder down the stairs. She snuggled down under the covers and let her mind drift over her shopping trip with Julia.

They had gone to the store after lunch at a trendy new place with uncomfortable little tables crammed too close together and a menu on which everything came dusted with bacon. Kendra, who had been halfheartedly trying to lose the baby fat that still clung to her hips and thighs four years after the twins were born, ordered the falafel salad. Julia ordered a bacon cheeseburger served on two doughnuts.

"Oh, my God, Julia, that's the most disgusting thing I've ever seen," Kendra said when their meal came. "How can you eat like that and weigh, what? Ninety-eight pounds?"

Julia had always been exquisitely tall and thin, with straight dark hair and sharp eyebrows. Kendra, by contrast, was her short, plump sidekick, with a halo of unruly red frizz and a childish sprinkling of freckles.

Julia shrugged a bony shoulder. "High metabolism." She dredged a pair of french fries through a little cup of habanero mayonnaise and folded them into her mouth. "Also, no kids."

Julia was Kendra's last remaining childless friend. The rest had either joined the ranks of harried parents, or drifted out of Kendra's life as she became too busy and tired to hang out. But Julia continually towed Kendra off the mommy shoals and back into the current of life.

After lunch, the two walked down a narrow, cobbled street, poking into boutiques along the way. Kendra did very little gift-buying and a lot of looking at things she couldn't afford, and which would get broken within two days of coming into her home even if she could afford them.

"Let's go in here," Julia said, hooking her arm around Kendra's and tugging her through an open doorway between two glass-fronted stores and up a dingy gray staircase that smelled of stale cigarette smoke.

At the top of the stairs, Julia turned to a wooden door with a small black sign engraved with "Inanna's Descent" in bright teal letters. A card taped to the edge of the door read, "No one under 18 years of age admitted." Julia pushed the door open and pulled Kendra inside.

"Jesus, Julia, are you kidding me?" Kendra hissed as she stepped into the room. Stacked on a table near the door were several small boxes and a hand-lettered sign that read, "Christmas Special: Cock Rings 15% Off."

"Calm down," Julia said, not bothering to lower her voice. "It's a feminist toy shop. Let's just look around. You might find a stocking stuffer for Charlie. Or for yourself."

"What does that even mean, 'feminist toy shop'?" Kendra whispered, her eyes still fixed on the boxes of cock rings. But Julia had wandered across the shop and didn't appear to hear her.

"Let me know if I can help you with anything." A young woman stepped forward and smiled at Kendra. Dressed in a plain green sweatshirt and jeans, with pale blue eyes, skin that looked skimmed off the milk pitcher, and white-blond hair pulled back in a ponytail, she looked like she'd just stepped off a Midwestern farm rather than out from behind a display of dildos.

"Okay, thanks," Kendra said, her voice wavering an octave higher than normal. She turned to a wall lined with books and pulled a volume at random from the shelf. As she flipped through it her eyes were greeted by men and women lying on beds draped with white linens in front of big windows looking out on serene landscapes and blue skies. The tanned and white-toothed couples smiled as they demonstrated various sexual positions, each one more awkward and uncomfortable-looking than the last.

Now, in bed alone, with the boys and Charlie downstairs, Kendra pictured the couples in the book again. Their bodies were too perfect, the poses ridiculous, and the settings unrealistic. But maybe--just maybe--sex could be as fun as their too-white smiles implied. Kendra let her legs slide apart and felt down between them, the soft, scant fur, the warm wetness. Her flesh was still tender, tingling from Charlie's work. She strummed tentatively, feeling her way around the unfamiliar territory of her own body. She couldn't remember how long it had been since she'd touched herself in a non-medical fashion. Taking care of herself in any manner had fallen to the wayside, both because she had so little time and energy and because, on some subliminal level, self-care equated with selfishness. Self-pleasure was out of the question.

Back in the store, she had shoved the book back on the shelf and hurried over to where Julia stood inspecting a small brown bottle. Nearby, a man and woman, the only other customers, held up between them a purple leather thing that looked like a dog harness. The man lifted another leather thing—was it a *whip?*—off a hook and held it out to the woman. She nodded her head, fingering the orange braided leather. They looked almost as old as Kendra's parents, yet here they were weighing bondage options as if deciding between generic and name-brand cream cheese.

Kendra tore her eyes away from the harness couple and grabbed a bottle off the shelf in front of Julia. A tiny sticker on it said, "Try Me," and Kendra flipped the top and squeezed some onto her hands. It was sticky and smelled strongly of coconut.

"What is this stuff?"

"Lube," Julia said.

"Ugh." Kendra wiped her hands on her jeans. The last thing she needed was any more moisture *down there.* She hadn't practiced her Kegel exercises like she should have, and ever since the twins' birth, she had been in danger of wetting her pants with every sudden cough or sneeze.

Julia turned to a display that held dozens of little trays of things shaped like lightbulbs, balloons, beetles, sea urchins, and UFOs. Each tray was labelled: "The Tickler," "The Juicer," "The Restrainer," "The Stinger," "The Seismic Noodle." Packets of sparkly nipple pasties and tassels hung from hooks and ruffled panties in every color of the rainbow cascaded down one side of the display.

"How about a butt plug?" Julia asked.

"What?" Kendra gaped at the array before her, wondering where one was meant to stick a long rubber rod, ridged with bean-sized knobs every two inches.

"A butt plug," Julia repeated. "Would that excite you and Charlie?"

"I don't find assholes sexy."

"That's funny. You've sure slept with a lot of them."

It was true. Before she met Charlie, Kendra had dated a streak of self-centered, overbearing, and obnoxious men. Assholes every one.

"Have you been here before?" Kendra asked as she and Julia wandered toward the back of the shop.

"Well, you know," Julia said, pointing to a basket on the floor. "A single girl's gotta do what a single girl's gotta do." The basket was filled to overflowing with rubber penises, complete with scrotum sacks, in several shades of human flesh-tones. Kendra felt her falafel rise in her throat.

"Why," she asked, "would anyone want one of those?"

Julia pursed her lips and gave Kendra a look that said, *Don't be so naive.*

"I mean a prosthetic vagina, that I could see the point of," Kendra said. "I could just hand it to Charlie and go back to sleep. But a penis? God, I'm surrounded by enough of those already."

"You know, there are more kinds of sex in the world than married couple missionary position."

Kendra tried to picture her friend alone, making use of a rubber penis. But maybe she wasn't alone. Maybe she was with someone else, someone who didn't come already equipped. Did Julia's ever-rotating selection of lovers include women? Kendra wouldn't be surprised; Julia probably thought sticking to one flavor of sex partner boringly conservative. But did she also think Kendra was too conservative to tell her about that side of her life?

Ever since they had met in a life drawing class in college—Kendra had needed an art credit; Julia was the nude model—Julia had made it her mission to relieve Kendra of her conventions, introducing her friend to skinny dipping, strip poker, and pot-smoking that first semester. Although she'd never fully purged Kendra's prudishness, she hadn't given up trying.

Lying in bed, idly exploring herself, Kendra pictured the basket of penises and laughed. She still didn't want—or need—one of those. Charlie's was ready and waiting at pretty much any hour of the day. But Julia was right; there were more ways than one to enjoy sex.

"Of course, if a penis is not to your taste," Julia had said, "you could always give one of these a try." She motioned to the wall above the penis-basket, where vibrators of all sizes and colors hung from display hooks. Most of them were penis-shaped, but some of them looked like Medieval torture devices, with knobs, prongs, and protrusions, and many were shaped like animals—rabbits, snails, butterflies, wasps, piglets, squids.

Kendra tried to picture the scene. *Should we get out the rabbit to help move things along, honey? Oh, where is that damn rabbit?* They would find it under the bed, sex bunny consumed by dust bunnies, an old piece of Halloween candy stuck to its ears.

"The boys would think it was a light saber and play *Star Wars* with it," Kendra said. "I'd have to get two of them."

Julia grimaced. "Now *that's* disgusting." She turned to a nearby shelf where boxes of rubber ducks marched single-file. "How about one of these?" They looked like children's bath toys, only with elongated necks and tails, and came in Easter egg hues--pale pink, seafoam green, baby blue, lavender, and lemon. A bright orange sunburst on the top right corner of each box declared the toys "BPA- and Phthalate-Free!"

"Well, that's reassuring," Kendra said. "Non-toxic sex toys."

"You don't want any nasties in your love-box," Julia concurred.

Kendra tried to imagine what to do with such a thing. It was so toy-like it seemed perverse to employ it in the way intended. She pictured it sitting on the edge of the bathtub, lined up alongside the boys' toy boats and wind-up sharks. On the rare occasion that she had both the time for a bath and the energy to scrub out the tub, she took a book and a cup of tea in with her, and read until the water got cold and her toes shriveled up. Sex never entered the picture.

It wasn't that she didn't enjoy sex anymore; she just never thought about it. It was almost as if it had served its purpose, giving her two beautiful, rambunctious children, and she had no need of it anymore. But maybe, Kendra thought as she watched Julia revel in the delights the store offered, she was missing the point. She pulled a little pot of pink nipple-flavoring cream off a nearby shelf and sniffed it. It smelled exactly like the watermelon LipSmackers lip balm she had had as a child. Bringing back memories of being eight was not what it would take to put the oomph back in her sex life.

She wandered back to the book section and, glancing through the titles, picked up a book about having multiple orgasms. That could be a real time-saver, she thought. If she and Charlie could each orgasm four or five times whenever they had sex, they could cut back to once a month. She flipped through a few pages and saw that the first step in the program was for each partner to take the time to discover what satisfied his or her own body. She imagined sending the boys and Charlie to a Saturday afternoon movie or calling in sick to work, "I can't come in today. I need to spend some quality time exploring my erogenous zones."

But now she really was alone, for at least a little while. She slipped out of bed and locked the door. In the dresser mirror, she studied her body, forcing herself to see luscious curves and creamy skin, not saggy boobs and stretch marks. Taking a few deep breaths, she tried to remember the order of events from the orgasm book. *Top to bottom,* she recalled and put her fingertips to her scalp where they became entangled in the snarls of her hair. *Okay, skip the head.* She moved her fingers to stroke her own face, her neck, her arms, listening with one ear to make sure the boys stayed downstairs. She cupped her breasts and rolled her nipples between her fingers. In the mirror, she watched as a flush spread across her skin, part embarrassment, part arousal.

Goosebumps sprang up along her arms and legs—it was too cold in the old farmhouse to stand around naked—and her hands made a hurried survey of the rest of her body before she scurried back under the blankets. From a drawer in her bedside table she pulled a plain brown bag and dumped the contents out onto the bed: seafoam green, BPA-free rubber duck and amber bottle of organic lube. "Now what am I going to do with you?" she asked the duck. Deciding its tail end was slightly less perverted than its head, she squirted on a glop of clear gel and slipped it beneath the covers. She spread her legs and opened herself to the duck as it slid in and out, up and down, searching out and finding pleasure points she'd never known she had. She pictured her own body, pale and plump before the mirror; Charlie's face, the look of gratitude he always had after sex; Julia's silken hair and angular collar bone, her complete ease in her body. Images from the toy store flickered across her mind—whips and knobby rods and cock rings—most of it ridiculous but a few things it might not hurt to try out. A mood-setting lamp shade, for instance, or a pair of crotchless panties. And then she forgot about Charlie and Julia and the sex toy store. Forgot about the scribbles on the wall and the Playmobil on the bedside tables. Forgot that she was too tired and busy to care for sex. Forgot even that it was a green rubber duck moving rhythmically inside of her—tail-head-tail-head-tail-head—that was making her forget. She forgot everything but the waves of pleasure that radiated through her body, sent her writhing in the gritty sheets, and left her lying numb and tingling all over.

"Breakfast!" Charlie called from downstairs.

Kendra lay a moment longer, a faint smile curving her lips. She pulled the duck out from under the covers and looked it in the eye.

"Not bad for the first day on the job." She dropped it and the bottle of lube in the paper bag and tucked them back in the drawer. "Not bad at all."

Wrapping her bathrobe around herself, she unlocked the bedroom door and headed downstairs to eat breakfast with her family.

need

HOLLIS QUEENS

This wasn't how things were supposed to go. She had planned on heading upstairs to change into a sexy, lace camisole and light some candles, a ceremony to mark their first time coming together for a reason other than trying to conceive. But their need has outweighed their patience. Given the last three years, they have been patient long enough.

Their leather couch groans in pleasure as he shifts his weight onto her. She closes her eyes as his lips find hers with a rough kiss, insistent in its desire to awaken in her what has been released in him. A movie they have seen at least a dozen times carries on in the background, a soft cinematic glow playing out over their reclining bodies. She runs her hands up the muscles of his back, and he lifts long enough to tug his t-shirt over his head before returning to bury his head into her neck. Kissing his way down her clavicle, he works his hands up her shirt until it comes to rest on her breast and teases her nipple through the bra.

The baby monitor crackles to life on the coffee table, causing them to freeze as if they are teenagers and the radio is a turning doorknob, signaling a parent's return. The baby fusses for a moment, but grows quiet again as she drifts back to sleep.

He returns to her, his need having grown in the intermission. Hungry hands fight the buttons of her blouse until she is exposed, her pink sports bra looking vulnerable under his gaze.

His eyes stare at the white cotton panties as if what lies beneath is a treasure chest and not what she still thinks of as a barren tomb lined with the relics of life. His fingers trace the elastic border lightly before slipping past, as if testing to see if they are electrified. The cotton isn't, but his fingers are.

The cold metal of his wedding band shocks the sensitive flesh of her inner thigh. The foreign feeling of something other than latex gloves sends shivers down to the ankles hugging his knees.

Out of habit she braces herself for the immediate probe, the frantic search for the cause of her problems, as if the doctors' digits could cure her infertility if only they could reach far enough inside her. Instead, his fingers massage the fleshy folds, swollen with anticipation, the pink sponge seeping juice with every press. It has been so long since foreplay has been a part of their repertoire that even the kissing has her wet.

Tonight, it doesn't matter if she is ovulating or not. This moment is not about needing to, it is about them needing each other. He kneads her labia, massaging northward until he finds the sensitive knot of her clitoris with his thumb. Her back arches into the pillows as he teases, now both hands under the crotch of her panties as he works her little joystick, rolls her clit until the friction makes her eyes roll back in a pleasure so raw that she grabs his hands to stop the torture but grinds her hips to keep it going.

His fingers find freedom from the cotton confines, but she grabs his wrists and draws them to her mouth. She takes each finger and sucks off the salty brininess of her arousal. By the time she is on the last finger of his right hand, his left has worked its way to the back of her head, fingers snaking through her short bob. There is a slurpy pop as he withdraws from her mouth to work his sweatpants down his hips with spit-slick fingers.

She doesn't mind the force he uses to guide her head to the bulge in his boxers. After years of being treated as a fragile, broken thing, she welcomes the strong grip pushing her onto her hands and knees, guiding her face to the gaping fly while his other hand attempts to free his growing cock. It is already hard when he starts feeding it to her, pushing his erection past her lips so quickly that it takes her by surprise.

Blow jobs had gone the way of foreplay in their quest for a child, replaced by fad diets promising to boost fertility and painful shots to increase hormone production. She chokes him down just like she swallowed the tips and advice, to the root, savoring his taste. Her tongue explores his highway of veins, a once familiar path forgotten over the last three years.

A few minutes later, she is so into sucking him off that he has to tap her on the shoulder to get her attention.

"Slow down." He groans and thrusts his hips as she keeps up the pace. "Stop or I'm going to come."

His attempts to push her off him are half-hearted, and a few strokes later his cock spasms in her mouth, filling her throat. She swallows, sucks him clean before sitting up to kiss him.

Even with the baby upstairs, somehow it still feels wrong. She has to remind herself that there is no such thing as 'wasting valuable seed,' a phrase they had discovered online back in the day and had laughed about until the little blue lines weren't forthcoming and they had stopped laughing and sucking and doing anything else that stood between them and their child.

He removes the sticky boxers and gets her naked too before kneeling on the floor and returning the favor. She rests her head on an accent pillow and is just starting to relax when he pushes her knees up to her shoulders to gain access to her pink slit. The invisible stirrups take her back to the doctors, but instead of the cold sting of a speculum it's her husband's warm tongue lapping her lips, and she gets lost in the pleasure.

Whether it is his tongue or his slick fingers diving into her tightness (the one silver-lining in having a surrogate), she neither knows nor cares. The electrical circuits of her legs crackle at the attention, long-dead lines starting to show signs of life. A wet finger presses experimentally on her puckered hole, tense with neglect. He pauses. She shifts her hips down, impaling her ass on his fingertip.

He had popped her anal cherry on their first date and had continued experimenting until they started trying for children. From then on, only the front door was viable. They removed their shoes before entering, turned three times once in the door and did whatever other crazy things the internet told them they needed to do in order to conceive.

His tongue is doing triple time on her clit, two fingers deep in her twat and one buried in her ass when she comes for the first time. Nothing major, only a few sparks shooting down her thighs. The heaviness below her navel is still there like a weight she just can't shake, like baggage she can't let go of.

He pulls her to the floor, pushing aside the baby toys peppering the tan carpet. She grabs a pillow out of habit and starts to lie on her back, but he grips her shoulder and pulls her on top of him. She remembers an article about how gravity can hurt the chances of the little swimmers making it upstream, but the soft snores coming from the monitor on the side table help her forget all about the rules.

She positions his prick so that when she descends, the tip slips inside her. Bouncing on the balls of her feet, she dips down further, inching him through her walls, swollen with need. By the time she has him all the way in, her thighs are screaming, so she drops down to her knees.

He grabs her hips, pulls and pushes. He bends his legs and tries to lift his hips, tries to fuck her from below. Her legs grip him like a bull rider while he bucks and she bounces. They have been scheduling sex for years, but none of their practice seems to have paid off. The lack of synchronicity makes it feel like they are just thrashing around, fumbling in a sexual limbo that brings them no closer to release for all their efforts. The more they try and the further they reach, the more their orgasms elude them. He fucks her faster. She rides him harder. Finally, she falls on top of him, their chests heaving in unison from their exertions.

They laugh because it doesn't matter anymore. He doesn't need to come any more than she needs to lie with her hips tilted at the precise angle for an hour after sex.

She relaxes into him, their sweaty skin sticking their flesh together until she sits up again, peeling herself off him only to find this erection unphased by their pause. She would be content to clean up and go to bed, but he reaches for her breast and caresses its peak in such a way that she knows he wants to continue. His hand trails down her torso, but finds her tacky lips sealing the entrance shut.

"I can get the baby oil from the changing table," he offers.

She pauses and then nods in agreement before watching his erection bounce across the living room. He had suggested surrogacy or adoption after the first year, but she had held on to the dream of conceiving for another two years. He had submitted to her schedules and rules, had allowed her to use his body like a 24/7 bank, and now she would do the same for him.

The baby oil feels cold as he dribbles it down her crack. Bent over the sofa, she wiggles her bottom at him, making the stream drizzle over her ass like icing on a confection. His hand cups her pussy and wipes up her lips to catch the oil before it drips on the carpet. He massages it into her skin, squeezing her ample hips and cheeks, parting the flesh to reveal her hidden portals before pressing them together again. He takes turns sliding his fingers in both holes while he lubes his erection with his free hand.

When he finally replaces his fingers with his cock, there is no preamble. His first thrust is so hard that she grunts in surprise as if his head has bypassed her cervix and plowed into her diaphragm. She can feel his thighs on the back of hers as he pauses a minute, silently reclaiming this space inside her that she had reserved for another. Then he is taking her hard.

The sound of their skin slapping together echoes across the room, an auditory arousal, and she can feel her own lubrication mingling with the baby oil as he slams into her, a deep tissue massage from the inside out, breaking through the tension she has held onto for so long.

He pistons in and out as thoughts flash in her mind, images of her life as she had planned it. Marriage, house, baby – in that order.

His palm slapping high on her ass shocks her out of the slideshow stuck on replay. She reaches between her legs and starts working her fingers over her slick clit. Every time she tries to press harder, her target slips away. The need in her grows as does the frustration at not getting what she wants.

Her dream of having a baby has taken on a form of its own over the years, like a living, growing thing that she carries with her.

He picks up the pace and her free hand falls between the sofa cushions and bumps into something hard. Her fingers close around a rattle and its clanging sings out in time with the thwack of their sticky skin and throaty moans. He is getting closer, so she rubs herself more frantically in an effort to come. As if he can sense that she needs more, he circles her asshole with his thumb, increasing in pressure until he is past her rim and so far inside that he can probably feel his hardness pressing on the other side of the wall.

She has held on long enough: to her plans, her perceived failures, her orgasms. As the heaviness inside her seems to grow unbearable, she lets it all go. The rattle falls from her hand and crashes to the ground. Her pussy clenches around his cock so hard that it traps him inside her for a moment before releasing him along with a flood of her own juices. He loses himself on the next thrust and they ride out their orgasms as their wetness drools down their legs.

He slides out of her and pulls her onto the floor into a tight embrace where they cuddle in contented solitude until their baby cries out with needs of her own.

LUDA JONES

I could tell the events of Thursday evening were still eating at May as we walked through town, but she didn't say anything until we got to the comic club at the library. She hovered at the doorway, then drew back and launched into me like a cuddle-and-apologies missile.

"Oh love. It's alright." They say—They say a lot of things, don't They—that inevitably there will come a point where your kid won't be seen dead hugging you in public. May and I seem to have skipped it. It still might happen, but not today.

"Noooo," she wailed faintly into my armpit. "I was being stupid, I was being *silly*—" she spat the word with such venom against herself, because stupid's one thing but *silly*'s always followed by *little*, isn't it. And May, however much I tell her otherwise, feels like she can't ever be a kid. Like she can't burden me. I wrapped my arms round her.

"Shhh," I said. "You've earned being a bit silly." She bloody has too. I held her and felt her shoulders relax.

"Just wait till you're sixteen. The fact that the tattoo lady wasn't taking any of your lot's nonsense suggests to me that she runs a good shop, so you could go back to her if you wanted. But not for another three years, ok?"

"Ok."

"At least three years. You might not even want one by then." I pecked the top of May's head. "See you at three."

May went in to join the comic club. First Saturday of the month, a bunch of kids sitting around talking about superheroes, and feelings, and drawing things off the internet. Not like in my day. But then Saturdays in my day involved hanging around behind C&A copping off with various troubled youths and sniffing glue, so on balance I'm very glad of the comic club.

I headed out of the library and up the High Street.

I had called her "the tattoo lady" but it was piercings May and her mates were after. Their tongues, and parts beyond. Give me strength. The lady had asked for ID, of course, and Grace, who is always at the forefront of these types of goings-on, had "kicked off"—in May's words—and they were told to leave the shop.

Thinking of it now, I decide I want to talk to the tattoo lady. It's a nice shop, sells girly odds and ends too, good for stocking fillers and the like. I don't want to feel awkward going in there. So I should stop by and apologize, smooth things over. I know I don't have to. I just have this feeling that I should. Like a nudge in my body. I have learnt about listening to those.

I make my way down the hipstery side street that this tattoos and piercings shop is on. It's a long, skinny shop. There's all the makeup and jewelry in the front half, a knowingly naff neon sign —TATTOOS—over the bead-curtained doorway of the back half. A few people are in there, teenage girls and their mums or nans perusing the makeup. Behind the till, there's this woman. Is she the one they spoke to? Twentysomething, probably. Wearing a black t-shirt with writing on it which I can't make out, stretched as it is over her breasts and disappearing into folds under them and tucked sharply into high-waisted denim shorts. She's a big girl, as my old mum would've called her with a bit of a pitying look. Can't imagine this one letting anyone pity her for a second. She stands solid and takes up exactly as much space as she's meant to.

She leans over to give some kid her change. I loiter for a bit and pretend to read the nail varnish. Cherry. Chili. Corvette. I had my nails done the other day. Plum ombre, apparently. It's become a semi-regular thing. My cousin Karen comes round, I do us some lunch, she does my nails. Little things like that feel really precious now.

Coast clear. I go over to the woman. Trying not to gawp in open admiration at her hair. It's bleached and shaved at the sides. A little longer at the top and dyed the colours of a Zap lolly. Can you still get those?

"Hi," the woman says.

"Hello." Why am I doing Posh Voice? "Ah, my daughter and some other girls came in earlier in the week, they're thirteen—well, one of them's twelve—looking to get their tongues pierced—"

A change in her stance. I notice her hand shaking slightly and she moves it down quick to her side.

Oh no. She thinks I'm some old cow come to have a go at her for daring to deny my little princess anything.

"Right. Yeah," she says. "I remember them. The legal piercing age in the UK is—"

"Yes—yes of course—I only—I wanted to thank you. If I had known they were planning that I..." Oh no. She thinks I'm some abusive bitch who's gonna go home and give the child a leathering for a perfectly normal bit of teenage rebellion. "I mean, I would have been very disappointed, so I'm grateful for you stepping in. Thank you." Oh no. I can't stop thinking about the terrible things she just *must* be thinking about me, which means I fancy the arse off her.

She smiles at me. Looks at me properly. Like steel shutters behind her eyes starting to lift.

"No need to thank me. I'm not gonna do tongue piercings on a bunch of little girls, from a moral or legal standpoint."

"Still—"

Someone else approaches to buy some lipstick. I shift out of the way.

There was May's dad...and then there wasn't. There was the odd girlfriend or boyfriend when May was little, whom she accepted with the matter-of-fact kindness which is one of the loveliest things about her. Then I was single for a long time, and then, cancer.

I get a lot of history stuff out of the library. Lately I've been reading about people living through the Blitz, shagging like rabbits because they could all be dead tomorrow. Maybe it works like that during wartime, I don't know. I only know that when there was the distinct possibility of my death hanging about the place, I didn't feel at all horny. Just scared. Just sick as a dog and weak as virgin's piss.

And at the same time, furious. Not at Fate or God or any of that, but at myself. That I might conk out. Not be there for my May. So all of me went into making sure I was. And after that, into being the Mum she'd missed out on, when she'd had to look after me.

It's been a while, is what I'm saying.

I look up at the neon sign. A tattoo really is something I've been thinking about, it's not just the proximity of this woman and her spiky softness or soft spikiness which is doing things to me.

To my left, a group of girls march out the door like they're going to war. Another group linger and drift but do eventually leave so that the shop, for now, just now, is empty. Fuck it. Fuck it, just say it. Lay it out.

"Do you do mastectomy tattoos?"

She doesn't wince. "Yeah. We certainly can do. I've only ever done one, myself. There's a lady who's way more of an expert than me, who's based in Sheffield, but she does come over here quite often. I mean, something like that, course, it's not usually like an off-the-peg tattoo sort of thing, we tend to do quite a bit of consultation first."

I swear it just comes out. "I'd like to consult you, if you're up for it." Oh bloody hell. What is this, *Confessions of A Uni-Titted Fortysomething Single Mum?*

"Would you?" I think it's called a Significant Look, the look she gives me. I'm still half-expecting her to tell me I'm worse than my daughter, order me out of the shop. But she smiles. Toys with her t-shirt in an endearingly—and intriguingly—shy way, because nothing else about her seems shy. She smiles down at her own fiddling hands.

"Well. It's only me in the shop right now. Do you want a quick consultation or something more..."

The radio is on in the shop, but it's quiet. So quiet, when she slides off the stool behind the till and steps forward I swear I hear her thighs *kiss*—

"...in depth?"

My mouth is suddenly dry as a hangover. It's happening. I'm—we're—making things happen. I nod. Steel shutters wide open. All those polite safe customer-service barriers all blasted away. Me and her looking at each other.

She walks to the front door, locks it, fiddles with the plastic clock on the WE'LL BE BACK AT sign. I wonder how much time she's putting on there. She pulls the blinds down. Walks back in no great rush. The flesh between the bottom of her shorts and the tops of her rose-patterned over-the-knee socks flashing towards me in the half-light. She holds out her hand and we shake with a formality that would make me laugh, if I wasn't so nervy.

"Erin," she says.

"Debbie."

We go through to the back room, her first. Me enjoying the view.

It's clinical in the back room. Which is a good thing, obviously. Neat plastic drawers, a little sink with sickly green soap in a pump bottle, something that looks like an examination bed. But the examination bed's covered in red leather, and there's also an old sofa, and opposite the sofa is a full-length mirror with a frame made of rubber tentacles. That must be Erin's bag on the sofa. A satchel like the suck-up kids when I was at school. Oxblood leather all battered and scarred. Bet it feels soft. I focus on all of those things and stomp on the bad memories.

"What kind of thing do women tend to get?" I ask, looking round at the pictures on the walls of every conceivable flower and beast and bird and God knows what.

"Well every woman's different, course, and it's not even just women who get them, but for a lot of women, their breasts are, like, tied up—I mean, tied in—with their sense of their own womanhood, and self-love…"

I nod. I get that. But mine were mosquito bites and then they turned into spaniel's ears and then one of 'em tried to kill me. Not much love lost there.

"So people tend to go for…floral images, you know, that sort of symbolism. Hope, renewal, memory, beautiful things."

"What if I don't want it to be beautiful?" I say, surprising myself with the edge in my voice. "Why would I want it to be beautiful? Be a bloody joke, wouldn't it, if the first time I liked my tits was after…"

I look at the floor, the sparkling lino. The fish tank in the corner makes a bubbly noise.

Erin says, "Scary clown?"

I can't laugh because I think it would turn into a sob, so I look up and say "Yeah. Red eyes."

"Fangs," she says.

"Yeah. Dripping with blood."

"Torn flesh."

"Maggots."

We're kissing. Tongues and hands everywhere, like teenagers. She unbuttons my blouse. I drag it off. She reaches round to the clasp of my bra—then stops and steps back.

"Sorry. I didn't think," she says quietly. "You don't have to, if you don't want. I used to leave everything on, when I was younger. Except the light."

I drop my bra on the floor at her feet.

She pulls her t-shirt out where it was tucked into her shorts. I can see what it says now: IN LOVING MEMORY OF WHEN I GAVE A FUCK. She pulls it over her head.

Erin is, of course, covered in tattoos. Flowers, pin-ups. A robot heart above her own. A magpie high on each thigh.

I lift her bra off. Her breasts are young and amazing. I lift one in two hands and suck the pink-brown nipple which is wider than the widest my mouth can get. I'm not thinking about me. How bad I look. I'm thinking about how good I feel, we feel.

I unbutton her shorts. Once they're a puddle round her ankles I start at her knickers. She helps me, looking greedily at my nails, which are things of beauty to be fair. She thrusts herself at me.

"Do it," she says. "I love getting fucked by straight girls, you mess me up inside for days after—"

"Who are you calling straight, you cheeky cow?"

"Sorry."

I put a witchy finger on the tip of her nose. "I think you're messed up inside enough as it is."

She grins.

I walk her back against the red leather bed thing. Peel her black cotton pants all the way down, till she can kick them away along with her shorts. I am weirdly relieved that we're both wearing boring knickers. I kneel, and part her magpie thighs. She has silvery stretch marks there, catching the light like a swimming pool.

I kiss her, once. She moans. I reach my hands across the dimpled expanse of her arse, rake her gently with my nails as my lips pluck at her clit. Then not so gently. She rattles out a whispery *yes-yes-yes* that I feel in the pit of my stomach and grabs my hands to press my nails further into her. I give her what she wants, lavishing her with cruelty and kisses till she comes in an opera of fluttery screams rising up up up, with one of her ballet pumps kicked off and her socked foot hammering on my shoulder.

Erin catches her breath. She looks down at me. It's a nice view, the smile of her belly, the rise of her breasts. There's worlds to her.

She lifts me to my feet, kisses me across to the little sofa. I kick my shoes off and start tugging down my jeans. Both her hands on me. I feel the thick numb lack of the scar tissue, and shuddery life on my whole breast, and between them my heart going, going like mad, still.

But when she starts kissing daintily down my ribs, I don't want it. I don't want all clever lips and tongues, I want bones, dexterity. "I want you inside me," I whisper to her. It sounds corny, Mills and Boonish. Not that she seems to mind. She drops into a sitting position between my splayed legs.

I can smell us both. Our fingers link below my belly for a second. My long nails and Erin's tiny nails with fingerflesh swelling around them. Well-worn blue varnish like little pools in the middle of each. She slips one finger into me and perfect randy frustration just about clenches me up. One?!?

More, more. I hold her hand between mine, give it a gentle tug, and she nods, understands, slips the second right in, and the third. Still not enough. I think of a foul joke I overheard some little lad tell the other day—*What's the difference between your Mum and a bowling ball? You can only get three fingers in a bowling ball*—and recalling it now, I laugh. Proper Carry On cackle. She doesn't seem fazed. She laughs too. Pushes in another.

I start to flush and tremble at the feeling of all four of her fingers crammed inside me. She curls them, a long slow *here-kitty-kitty*.

"More," I say.

"Serious?"

I think of the scar, the sour-faced smirk where my left breast was, think of my Nan's favourite saying, *We'll be a long time dead*, and I say "Do as you're told."

"Yes Miss." She reaches with her other hand into her bag and brings out what you could mistake for one of those little bottles of hand sanitizer, but it isn't, it's lube. She carries lube around in her bloody swot's satchel, of course she does. I'm giggling like a prat again – till I gasp at the cool drizzle of it.

She dallies, for a while, moving a little way out, a little way in, her dreamy soft-hard hands working with the lube and my wetness and there's plenty of both. My head tilts all the way back as if to make more room. I feel her knuckles, I feel impossibly stretched, at the very edge of pain, and then—

It's not a laugh exactly that she lets out, more of a quick, happy sigh. It sounds like amazement, discovery. "Look at that."

I sit up on my elbows and look in the mirror behind her. Her whole entire hand is in me. My cunt is hugging her wrist, like a weird flower opened to some hummingbird or bee, as open and as full as you can get.

I feel her move her hand, drawing her fingers down into a fist round her thumb. She talks me through it like a magician. Ta da.

She rubs my clit with her free thumb. I feel her everywhere, I feel her in ways that don't even make sense—inside on my clit, outside in my cunt—building a kind of ache like a glorious bruise. I almost can't stand it, it's almost scary. But I've been scared. So I'm saying "Yes." I'm saying "Yes yeah *fuck God MORE DO IT—*"

When I was a kid I used to come without knowing what it was. I used to come in my sleep sometimes. It hits me like that now, the sheer surprise of it, I'm rising and whooshing, I'm going over Niagara, sounds coming out of me I've never heard.

Then I'm coming down, slow, back to myself. To Erin's gentle voice telling me she's going to pull out, and she does, taking her time, talking all the while, but I still gasp to feel the sudden lack of her where I was so very full.

I look down at her between my legs. There's wet on her nose and cheeks and lips. Was she licking me when I went off?

She cracks a big goofy grin. "Aren't you supposed to say 'that's never happened before'?"

"What?"

"When you shoot your wad in a girl's face?"

"What?"

She has to spell it out. "You squirted."

"That never has happened before!"

"Serious?" She cleans herself like a cat, wiping her face with the side of her hand and licking it. "Well. It was 'mazing."

"Yeah it was." I lie back and conk out for a bit. She nips off, to the toilet I suppose. There's a clock on the wall. I've got another fifteen minutes till I have to go and meet May. Maybe half an hour if I leg it. I touch myself, strange and new. Wondrously open. We can still surprise ourselves.

Erin comes back to see me prodding the cushion under me, which is kind of squishy.

"Covers needed a wash anyway," she says. She perches next to me. "Is this ok?"

This girl. She's just had her hand up me and she's asking if it's ok for us to cuddle. You might think it would be awkward, our wild bodies plus the big stain I've made on this little sofa, but we fit fine. I sling an arm round her shoulders.

And we talk about the tattoo I could have. I tell her it would have to curve, it would have to flow in a lot of directions but all of them upwards. It would be sweet and weird and good. It would be beautiful. Some kind of rocket fueled by itself, gushing sugar and cream, feather and fire. An ice cream phoenix. All the colours of a Zap lolly.

hook and tink

BRANDY FOX

As Lance and I settle in with the kids for Family Movie Night, nooky is the last thing on my mind. Call me crazy, but spending time with two wild preschoolers doesn't usually put me in the mood. After twelve hours of shuttling, schlepping, cajoling, cleaning and cooking, I'm beat.

It's Peter's choice tonight, so of course we're watching *Peter Pan*. The five-year-old wears his green tunic and red-feathered cap, swatting the air with his sword while his little brother Garrett makes an island of pillows and blankets on the floor. Lance and I take either end of the couch, our legs entwined under a blanket.

I press play on the remote and watch Peter fly around the room, then land on the island with legs splayed and sword drawn. It's amazing how much he takes after his dad. Lance perpetually looks like he's on his way to a Renaissance Faire, with his long dark locks, hemp shirts that flow from his tall, lanky frame, and a memory for Shakespearean soliloquies he spouts at random moments. Sometimes it feels like I'm parenting three boys, not two. But there are times even I can't resist Lance's infectious energy.

Today, though, nothing's going to stop me from catching a few Z's during the movie. I'm dozing before Peter Pan's even taught the little ones how to fly.

"Poppycock!" Lance shrills suddenly.

I open my eyes to see him smiling broadly at me, then shoot him a warning glare. Soon I'm drifting off again.

Not long goes by before there's something wiggling against my thigh. My eyes whip open to see Lance with Captain Hook's own wicked grin, clearly amused by my exhaustion. He tickles my thigh with his toe again, wiggling his eyebrows at the same time.

I look down at the boys. As usual, the movie has put them in a trance. They're buried up to their necks in blankets, eyes glazed over as Peter Pan sprinkles pixie dust over the kids despite Tinker Bell's disapproval. I can see the wheels in my own Peter's mind turning, no doubt scheming how he could get himself some of that magic powder. He'd probably try it on Garrett first, who's willing to jump out a window if his big brother tells him to.

I look back at Lance. "Grow up," I joke.

"I don't want to grow up," he pouts.

"Head to Neverland, babe. You won't grow up there."

"Come with me," he says with a breathy, French accent. "I am thinking a wonderful thought."

I snort, turn on my side and try sleeping again. But as I drift off, I envision Lance with Captain Hook's wild mustache, ruffled blouse and long red coat, two cigars dangling between his lips. Surprisingly, I get a little slick in the groin.

Instead of sleeping, I watch the movie and let my mind wander. I'm guessing Lance would enjoy seeing me in that flimsy pixie dress. I barely clear five feet, and would have the same trouble as Tinker Bell getting my hips through a keyhole. Luckily, Lance adores my love handles, embraces and praises them with his rich vocabulary.

Next to tall, skinny Lance, I could be Tink. For the first time, her jealousy of Peter Pan's affection for Wendy strikes me as silly. I'm thinking Tink should just abandon him altogether and hook up with the Captain. He's certainly got the bigger bulge.

It's about when Captain Hook is plotting Tiger Lily's capture that I feel his big toe slithering up my thigh again. This time, though, instead of tickling, it weaves into my little fantasy of Hook and Tink getting it on, and I spread my legs in welcome.

"A little persuasion might be in order," Captain Hook says to Smee, and I'm thinking, *No, actually, it's not.* I look over at Lance. He's peering at me through slits, his head lolling against the armrest, his face full of both pleasure and concentration.

When his toe snakes its way up my inner thigh, I'm grateful to be wearing my loose-fitting nighttime garb: a pair of Lance's boxers and a t-shirt. The suspense is just about killing me and by the time his toe brushes against my labia, I'm on fire. I scoot my hips eagerly closer. His toe finds my swollen clit and caresses it, impressing me with its precision despite being the inferior digit. I circle my hips and suppress a moan even though our fancy sound system would certainly drown it out. Besides, the boys are so immersed in the movie they wouldn't notice an earthquake.

When the mermaids appear onscreen, Lance opens his eyes to watch. His mouth goes slack and he licks his lips. I had a feeling he got turned on by all those scantily clad mermaids with star-cup bras and flowing hair, not to mention the cat fight they have with Wendy. I decide it's his turn for some fun, so I slide my own foot up his leg and find his sword ready for a duel. I wrap the arch of my foot across his bulge and stroke up and down its length. I can feel Lance squirm, making a half-assed effort to be discreet.

It goes on like this for longer than I thought possible: Lance's toe massaging my nether region while my foot pets his. My hand finds its way inside my t-shirt to cup my breast, notching up the pleasure and making my belly clench with the hot pressure of it all.

When Peter Pan is named Flying Eagle by the Chief and everyone but straight-laced Wendy joins in on the dancing and pipe-smoking, we notice something's amiss. Usually in this scene, our boys are up and dancing along with the Lost Boys, but tonight they're comatose. Lance must figure they're asleep, because abruptly he removes his toe and sits up. He repositions the blanket around himself like a cape and comes in for the kill.

I shake my head. There's no way I'm doing it on the couch with our kids just feet away from us, awake or asleep. But Lance won't take no for an answer. He looks around the room as if searching for a more private location to move this match. Then his eyes brighten with what I'm sure he believes is a brilliant idea. He takes my hand and abandons ship, dragging me with him.

He doesn't take us far: just behind the couch. I open my mouth to protest, but Lance's tongue darts in and traces my lips, then finds my tongue eagerly awaiting its arrival. Soon his mouth is moving down my neck, his hands inside my shirt to pinch my taut nipples, and I've forgotten what it was I wanted to protest. He lifts my shirt to keep his mouth moving down, down, down the length of my belly, over my mound. I stand up and lean my arms on the back of the couch to see that the boys are still sleeping. Plus it opens up the crotch of my boxers so Lance can have better access to my drenched pussy. His tongue goes straight for it, that exquisite, muscular, juicy tongue alternating between strokes and thrusts, again and again, making it nearly impossible to hold in the moans and gasps that normally flow freely.

At last, Hook and Tink are together. As Lance takes me to Neverland, Hook flirts with Tink on screen, weaving piano notes and smooth talk until Tink is gladly dancing across his map, swaying her supple hips en pointe. Knowing this is probably one of Lance's favorite parts, I push his head away and motion for him to kneel. As soon as he sees the screen, a smile breaks across his face. I tug his sweats down and unsheathe his sword, catching it in my mouth and devouring it. He shudders, reaches forward to steady himself on the back of the couch, then glues his eyes to the television.

When Hook locks Tink up, Lance once again takes command. He pulls himself away and twirls me around to face the screen. I squat as he caresses my asscheeks, teasing my begging cunt with a probing finger. After an excruciating moment, he replaces the finger with his rock-solid cock and it slides directly to my G-spot. Knowing I won't be able to keep quiet, Lance claps his hand over my mouth. He wraps his other arm around my waist so he can finger my nub while pulling my hips toward his as he thrusts. It takes every ounce of discipline to keep from screaming with the pleasure of him filling me up, like tiny Tink getting fucked from behind by the well-endowed Hook.

Within moments, every inch of my torso explodes, from my pulsing vadge to my puckering nipples. Hot waves roll up my body and I imagine pixie dust showering the room. I open my mouth to scream but Lance's hand only clamps tighter, so instead the scream vibrates through my throat and chest. Just as the fireworks end for me, Lance stops moving and presses his palm harder into my belly so that he's reaching deep inside me. I can feel his cock contract, his warm juices fill me up, and then his body go slack.

When Lance pulls himself away and releases me from his grip, I come to my senses. In the world outside of Hook and Tink's tryst, I hear Wendy begin her lullaby to her brothers and the Lost Boys. "A real mother is the most wonderful person in the world." Lance pulls up his sweats and wraps his arms around me. I lean my spent body back against his and let him rock me slowly, sweetly, his chin resting on top of my head.

Now that the lusty woman in me is satiated, I am once again Mother. I want to be cuddled up with my boys, too. I stand on tiptoe to kiss Lance, then come around the couch and snuggle in with the kids on the floor. Their eyes flutter open and blink sleepily. Lance snuggles in, too, all of us making a giant love nest. Everyone is drawn in by Wendy's song: the Lost Boys, the Indians, even Smee with his mother-heart tattoo. And our family, shamelessly weepy and cuddly until the song is over and Peter Pan warns, "Once you grow up, you can never come back" and I think, *You're wrong about that, Pan. Even horny adults can sneak off to Neverland every now and then.*

Sara Dobie Bauer is a writer, model, and mental health advocate with a creative writing degree from Ohio University. She lives with her husband in Ohio, although she'd really like to live in a Tim Burton film. She is a member of RWA and author of the paranormal rom-com *Bite Somebody*.

Cecilia Duvalle lives near Seattle with her husband, kids, and cats. Her short stories appear in multiple anthologies. She is also editor for Cwtch Press' series *Blood in the Rain*, a yearly anthology celebrating erotic encounters with blood-sucking creatures of the night. She can be found at www.ceciliaduvalle.com.

Luda Jones loves riotously happy, breathtakingly kinky queers, and writing filthy little stories about same. She has previously written some smut for Supposed Crimes' *Downpour* anthology (because what's sexier than rain?), and Exhibit A's Great British Bake Off erotica contest (because what's sexier than cakes?)

Andrea Lani is a writer, naturalist, and mother to three boys. Her fiction has appeared in *Literary Mama, Saltfront,* and *Brain, Child.* She received her MFA from the University of Southern Maine's Stonecoast program, is an editor at *Literary Mama,* and can be found online at www.remainsofday.blogspot.com.

Samantha Luce is a native Floridian. While she was hooked on strong women growing up in the eighties, watching Sarah Connor & Ellen Ripley, it wasn't until she reached her thirties that she finally embraced her inner lesbian. Now, she's making up for lost time by writing erotic short stories.

Jordan Monroe is delighted to be using her English degrees. She enjoys both listening to and playing music, watching *Sherlock* while anxiously waiting for new episodes, and buying too many books to fit on her bookshelves. She lives within 25 miles of Washington, DC.

Jennifer D. Munro is a freelance editor whose work has appeared in two editions of *Best American Erotica; Best Women's Erotica;* seven editions of *Mammoth Book of Best New Erotica; The Bigger the Better the Tighter the Sweater: 21 Funny Women on Beauty and Body Image;* and many other publications. Website: JenniferDMunro.com. Blog: StraightNoChaserMom.com.

Delilah Night is the mom of two exhausting daughters. Check out her novella, *Capturing the Moment,* and her stories in over a dozen anthologies including *Prompted, Nine to Five Fantasies,* and *Intrepid Horizons.* In 2016, Delilah edited her first anthology, *Coming Together: Under the Mistletoe.* Find out more at delilahnight.com.

Pooja Pande is a writer and editor based out of New Delhi, India, with a keen interest in culture and gender. Her first book, *Red Lipstick,* a literary-styled memoir on the life of celebrity transgender rights activist Laxmi, published by Penguin-Random House, came out in August 2016.

Hollis Queens is a longtime lover of erotic literature who is currently studying the writing craft in University of Tampa's MFA program.

J.A. Reed is a twenty-something year old writer in Northern Virginia.

Teresa Noelle Roberts started writing stories in kindergarten and hasn't stopped yet. A prolific author of short erotica, she's also known for erotic romances—paranormal, kinky contemporary and science fiction. Teresa enjoys belly dance, yoga, cooking, hiking, and organic gardening. She thinks she'd enjoy sleeping but it takes so much time!

Kristina Wright is a freelance writer and the editor of over a dozen erotic romance anthologies. Her short erotic fiction has appeared in over 100 anthologies. She lives in Virginia with her family and spends a lot of time in coffee shops. Find out more at kristinawright.com.

about the editor

Brandy Fox discovered the joys of reading and writing erotica when, as a mother of two young boys, a raging libido blew in and refused to let up until she paid attention to it, as well. Her erotica has appeared in *Women in Lust*, *The Mammoth Book of Quick & Dirty Erotica*, and *Hungry For More*. Her favorite stories address the myriad changes that come with motherhood, especially regarding sexuality, so it only made sense to gather a collection of them to share with the world. During daylight hours, Brandy is a sexuality educator, writing mentor, and youth advocate. She lives near Seattle with her kids and preternaturally good looking hunk of a spouse.